# STICKS AND STONES

A NOVEL

Dianne Beck

FROM THE TINY ACORN . . .
GROWS THE MIGHTY OAK

*Sticks and Stones*


Printed in the United States of America. For information, address
Acorn Publishing, LLC, 3943 Irvine Blvd. Ste. 218, Irvine, CA 92602

www.acornpublishingllc.com

Cover design by Damonza.
Interior design and formatting by Debra Cranfield Kennedy



Library of Congress Control Number: 2020932842

ISBN-13: 978-1-947392-82-3 (paperback)

*For my loving husband, beautiful children,*

*supportive family, dedicated friends and students,*

*all who gather sticks or stones or flowers or leaves, and*

*for the God who loves us all through and through.*

# STICKS AND STONES

# —1—

I have to get my mom out of jail. She's Tiffany Greene, the one who sang me to sleep when I was four, brought my dying pet goldfish back to life when I was seven, stayed up all night with me to make a model of a California Mission with homemade dough when I was nine.

Now that I'm fifteen, she's the only real family I've got, and she's not capable of committing a crime. She's too nice. Richard Holder, her fiancé who recently moved in with us, is the one who should be in jail. But at six in the morning, when the police knocked on our front door, Richard was conveniently missing.

I woke up to fists pounding on the front door that winter morning, shouting voices, "Police! Open up!" Next, the scurry of Mom's slippers, the opening and closing of cabinets and drawers, my mom's voice, high-pitched and frantic.

"I need to talk to my daughter. Please let me talk to her."

I sat up in my cozy, pillow-filled bed, rubbed my eyes to see if I was dreaming. Mom appeared in my doorway. She wore the long T-shirt she always wore to bed, green sweats with my Chaparral High track team logo on the side, and her black coat with the furry Sherpa lining I always loved. It was clear that she just threw on whatever was in easy reach. She swung her head to flip her tousled brown hair out of her green eyes. Everyone said we looked so much alike, more like sisters than mother and daughter.

But now, with her wrists handcuffed behind her, and her pretty face twisted in grief, it was impossible not to feel like we were both losing everything in an instant. *What was happening?*

"Okay, say what you need to say." The stocky policeman refused to look at me. He kept his eyes on Mom. Jared, my closest friend and also, unfortunately, Richard's son, ran in behind her.

"What's going on?" Jared's crystal blue eyes blazed. His hands grabbed Mom's petite shoulders. "Tell us what's happening!" At six foot two, he made her look so tiny, so fragile. His anger made him seem even larger.

"Jared, Emily, I'm so sorry. Call my mother—tell her you need to stay with her."

Mom stared at Jared, like she was expecting him to understand and follow her orders. In the awkward stillness that followed she said, "That's all I can tell you right now, I'm sorry."

Jared's chest heaved up and down like he'd been running, his mouth quivered. "Yeah, whatever, I've heard that line before. Us kids aren't allowed to know anything, but we still have to live with all your problems."

"I love you guys. You're the best, okay? Please remember I love you and um, know that I'm sorry." Tears showered her face.

I hated seeing her helpless, unable to even wipe her tears because of her cuffed hands, or to make things better for us like she always did. I knew this couldn't be her fault. My mom was a good mother. She worked long hours as an emergency room nurse. We lived in a nice home, in a quiet neighborhood, in beautiful Southern California. Things like this didn't happen to families like ours. "Why are you letting them take you? Where's Richard? Why aren't you fighting back?"

She looked down at her feet, opened her mouth like she

wanted to say something, but nothing came out. I ran to her, wrapped my arms around her waist. I breathed in her scent, a mix of her bath soap and vanilla perfume, felt a tear fall on my arm. I put my finger on that tear and let it soak into my skin where it would stay with me.

When the police officer pulled Mom away, I tried to hang on. I clung to her as long as I could, until they wrenched her out of my arms. Jared still stood there with his arms hanging down, his hands clenched tight into fists that might flail and punch if one more thing triggered them. The police officer led Mom out of my room.

I wanted to run down the hallway and pull her back, scream and tell the police they'd made a big mistake. I stared at all the things in my room that had her touch on them, the stuffed animals she bought me, the comforter of bright pink and green she bought when we redid my room, the pair of Reef flip flops I borrowed because we now wore the same shoe size. I wanted to hold it all close so no one could take any of it from me. I slipped on the flip flops, grabbed the white, plush lamb that felt like her coat. I felt like a four-year-old who lost her mom in the store. I held the lamb and the tears would not stop.

Finally, Jared moved. He wrapped his arms around me, held me tight. His shirt was the same soft cotton as Mom's sleep shirt. Even though he was only sixteen, he was strong, and present, and honest, and real. I didn't have a dad to turn to. He'd disappeared from our lives when I was a baby. Thank God I had Jared.

"Emily?"

I peeked out from Jared's arms to see a tall police woman with short black hair.

"I'm Officer Bankes." She extended her hand to give us a business card. "My number is on this card. I went ahead and called your grandmother, Emily, per your mother's request. She said you can both stay with her, unless you have another relative you want to stay with, Jared. No one seems to be able to get in touch with your father."

Jared's mother was dead. He never mentioned any other relatives.

"I'd like to stay wherever Emily is," he told the officer.

I was relieved he wanted to stay with me, even though I knew he could have gone with another friend to wait for Richard. I stared at the card with Officer Jena Bankes in dark blue lettering underneath the Chaparral County police department logo. Unless it was a get out of jail free card, I didn't really want her number.

I remembered dressing up like a police officer when I was in first grade. That costume had been the number one thing on my Christmas list that year. I told Mom that's what I wanted in October, after we had a community day at school and people came to talk about their jobs. The police officer who visited was a woman, and I thought she was the absolute coolest person ever. She stood in front of the class and told us that we should never be afraid to do what's right or to follow our dreams. She said that many people told her she couldn't be a police officer since she was a woman and only five feet tall. She became all the more determined by their put downs and proved them wrong. I loved that. Mom always told me I could be whatever I wanted to be, no matter what others said.

So when my police outfit arrived, complete with a dark blue vest, a shiny silver badge, handcuffs and a book of pretend blank tickets, I couldn't wait to put it on. I wore it every day, begged to wear it to school, but my mom said that wasn't allowed. I gave her a ticket for that, but it didn't change her mind. So I wore it the second I got home from school and had a blast handcuffing neighbor kids and passing out tickets to anyone who was mean. I would stare at myself in the mirror and imagine myself as the officer from school with her blonde ponytail, blue nail polish, and tough attitude who told us, "I became a police officer because I want to protect wonderful children like you, your families, your neighbors, and your teachers." I wanted that too, which was why I didn't understand how these people who were supposed to prevent bad things from happening were taking the best thing in my life away from me. I didn't get it.

I took Officer Bankes' card, folded it between my fingers into a tiny square, squeezed it as hard as I could to smash it, and tossed it on my bed when she wasn't looking.

For several hours we waited for Grandma while the police searched every room, gathered stuff in bags that they then sealed, offered us water, lunch. I had no interest in food. I was more interested in the fact that they hadn't found a single gun in the house. Richard was an obsessive collector. I never counted how many firearms he had because they always creeped me out, made me nervous, especially when he'd hold one and admire it like something he worshipped, and I had no idea if it was loaded. Yesterday before school I saw them all in Mom's bedroom, all lined up on the floor and on the bed. I was hoping he was getting rid of them, which now I see he was, along with disappearing from home right in time for the police to arrive.

Jared and I tried to pack only the necessities, for how long we didn't know. I hoped it was only a few days. My grandmother lived several hours away in Central California, some little town called Pine View, so there was no way I would get to school tomorrow. That really stressed me out since it was a Friday, the worst day ever to miss because nearly every teacher had a test or something due.

But even though I hoped for a short stay, I had a bad feeling it could be longer. I couldn't stand to leave some things behind, just in case. I packed all my journals filled with rants and poems and stories, the personal record pins I earned every time I took seconds off my eight hundred meter race in youth track, and the blue Nike shoes Mom bought me when I first started to run three years ago. They were way too small now, so worn they had holes, but they were the first pair Mom bought me. She saved money in a jar from working extra nursing shifts until she had enough money to buy them. I used to wear them everywhere, even to eighth grade graduation dinner with my fancy black dress. Yes, I looked dumb, but I didn't care. When they didn't fit anymore, I brought them with me to every track meet for good luck.

Each of my twenty-eight personal record pins reminded me I was seconds closer to beating the high school record and fast enough to be the league champion. If I did that, I'd have a shot at a college scholarship, hopefully to UCLA or UC Santa Barbara, two of my dream schools when I graduated in three years. Most people I knew would do almost anything over running to get through college. But for me, that's when I felt my best, like flying and fleeing all at once.

And my journals held my words, all the thoughts I needed to unload but couldn't speak out loud. They were like breath to me. When I didn't write them I felt heavy, suffocated.

The last thing I saw, staring at me from my desk, was my Bible, another gift from Mom. I touched its black leather edges, ran my fingers along the engraved lettering. I didn't want to pick it up. Unlike the words in my journals, I didn't know if I could trust these words. Maybe all those times of reading God, I could have been reading more J. K. Rowling, more S. E. Hinton, more John Green. Why had God left me without parents, left me with a sprained ankle right before Track season, left me alone? I decided the Bible didn't need to come with me.

We loaded Jared's truck with all our stuff, then we sat outside to wait for the grandmother I barely knew. Our neighbors got a good show while we sat and waited. Cars slowed down as they neared our corner house, peered out their windows to see why five cop cars lined the street. Kids stopped along their walk to school, pointed at us, confused looks on their faces. Not much happened in our quiet suburb of Chaparral. The only news coverage I remembered ever getting was when we were listed as one of the top five safest California cities. So, it was probably the first time most of the neighbors had seen a live crime scene.

After a while, Jared and I decided to sit behind the big mimosa tree where they couldn't see us. Jared laid his sweatshirt on the grass and we huddled together, hidden as we leaned against the wide tree trunk. This had become a regular spot for us not long after we met and became friends, before Jared's dad and my mom met, supposedly fell in love, and got engaged, making any chance of Jared and me being any more than friends sort of awkward.

I heard our neighbor, Mr. Calston, talking to a police officer, "What's going on? Is somebody hurt?" I could picture him peeking out over his thick, wide-rimmed reading glasses, his few strands of gray hair hanging over his forehead like my bangs did when they needed trimming. Mr. Calston had a talent for looking concerned while actually fishing for a good story to tell the world.

"No one is hurt, sir. But do you mind if we spend a few minutes asking some questions about your neighbors?"

"Great, of all people to talk to, we get him as our spokesman?" I told Jared.

I picked at the fuzzy flowers that fell from the tree and made our lawn more pink than green. Like everything I looked at, they made me think of my mom. She refused to cut down this tree in spite of it damaging our water pipes with its tangled roots. She hated how our feet carried half the tree with us, dragging it across the white tiled floors each time we entered the house. But she loved looking at it, sat at the table every morning with her hot coffee and gazed at it.

"I'll bet Mom doesn't have any pretty trees to look at in jail," I said.

Jared looked at me for a while before he came up with

something to say to that. "Probably not, but she'll find something good to look at, Em. She always finds the good in things."

That was true. She found whatever tiny bit of good there was in Jared's dad. They'd been engaged for a year, and I still hadn't figured out how to like him. But I still thought she would hate everything about jail. She took her time getting ready every morning, liked her quiet time before everyone was up and about, brought Clorox wipes to hotels to clean after the maids visited. Jail would be dirty, noisy, cold.

"You need to get in touch with your dad," I told Jared.

"I've tried him, about seven times, told him we're going to your grandma's. He's not picking up, not answering my texts. I don't think he will."

"Why wouldn't he respond? He needs to help us."

He just stared at me, wordless.

"I'll find him if you don't. I swear I will, no matter what it takes. He's not allowed to just bail on us. He knows something."

Still no words from Jared, which told me a lot.

I heard the rumble of a car engine, turned and saw a blue boat of a car inch behind the line of cop cars. "Looks like Grandma is here," I said. I blew the pink flower off my hand, watched it float and land, wished I could float away too.

# —2—

I didn't know why Mom chose Grandma to take care of us, even if it was just for a few days. I thought they weren't speaking to each other anymore. Every time they talked on the phone, they fought, and the last argument about a year ago sort of put an end to their talks. It was something about my dad. I often thought I should simply call him Landon or Mr. Sharpe, instead of Dad. It felt wrong to give a title like Dad to someone I'd never met.

"Mom, I don't need your help with Landon. He's the one that left, remember?" My mom shouted into the phone at Grandma. "I'm tired of you sticking up for him, going on about what God wants me to do, telling me all your nature stories. You sound crazy." She hung up, and I hadn't heard them speak since.

I didn't have a lot of interest in seeing the grandmother who was possibly crazy and nice to the father who left. Mom had told me I first met Grandma when I was three, sometime right after Grandpa died. I didn't remember that visit.

My memory of Grandma came from photo albums, pictures of her younger self in faded jeans and a dark bob haircut standing next to Mom, who looked to be about my age, fifteen. Mom had long, sleek brown hair and wore shorts with a plaid top, tied in the front to show her tiny tanned waist.

But the woman who stepped out of the old, blue boat of a car on the day of Mom's arrest did not look like the woman in those pictures, or a hippy, or a nature freak. She looked like a grandma. Gray fuzzy hair topped her slight frame. Her blue floral shirt matched perfectly with sky blue pants and a matching jacket.

"I wonder if her house is blue too," I said to Jared.

She squinted through the morning sunlight in our direction as I tried not to shiver in the brisk air.

"Jared? Emily? Is that you?" she called out.

"Yes, it's us," Jared said. He looked at me and patted my knee. "Okay, here we go, ready or not."

I took a deep breath, followed him to meet Grandma. She walked toward us with tiny little steps, her head peering down at the ground in front of her. She stopped, picked up something from the ground, took a few more steps, bent to pick up something else. When we got closer, I spotted a leaf and a stick in her hands. She tucked them into her purse, looked at us. I saw that her eyes were green like mine, like Mom's.

"I'm sorry about your mom," she said. Her eyes glistened with tears.

"We are too," Jared said.

I didn't know what to say. I felt so awkward. How could this be happening?

"Well, I'm glad you two are okay, and I'm happy to have you as long as you need." She reached her dainty hands out, held our hands in hers. They felt warm and soft. Then she shook hands with Officer Bankes, who stood nearby with papers in hand.

"We need you to sign a few papers." Officer Bankes said. "They basically say that you are taking the kids, that you're okay with phone calls or visits by us or social services, that you have shown us proof of identification and residency."

Grandma signed quickly, not too concerned about reading

the papers first. "So, when will we hear about Tiffany?" she asked.

"Well, Mrs. Greene, we are always available for you if you want to call us. These cases take some time. Do you have any specific questions right now?"

Grandma looked at us, turned so only Officer Bankes could see her face. "Is she guilty?" she whispered.

I hated when people whispered loudly, might as well just talk normal and give up trying to be secretive.

"I can't discuss too much of the case with you, but as the children know, we did arrest her on drug charges, possession, trafficking and distribution of controlled substances."

"Oh my, drugs, they really mess up people, their health, their spirit, their soul. She knows that. I can't believe she would do such a thing. Her father had a problem. I thought that would keep her away from drugs."

I wanted to yell at Grandma. Why did she assume Mom was guilty like everyone else here?

"I know this is a lot to take in right now. One of us will get in touch with you about counseling referrals for the kids and yourself."

"Counseling? I don't need a counselor. That's what got my husband stuck on drugs. They just gave him stuff so he wouldn't feel anything. Counselors are good people, but I need to trust in a higher power."

"I understand, ma'am. We certainly don't want damaging results from counseling. We just provide you with some names, won't make you go. It's just if you want."

Grandma reached into her purse, grabbed the stick and leaf, rubbed them between her fingers and closed her eyes before finally speaking again. "Thank you, officer. I know you're only trying to help." Grandma opened her mouth again, took in a deep breath like she was getting ready to say a whole lot more. But then she let out that breath, shook her head. "Uh, no, no, that's enough for today. I don't need to say any more. Just need to get these kids to my home, away from all this."

Jared and I climbed into his battered old pickup truck after Grandma gave us her address and directions. "We'll come back home, we'll come back home," I whispered to myself as we drove away.

# —3—

We followed Grandma's car through miles of orange groves, cow pastures, and dry hillsides. Jared and I imagined what Grandma's house would be like. We clung to one, small, positive hope that her home might be like those we saw on television or read about in fairy tales.

"Maybe she'll give us warm cocoa every morning, create homemade meals that cook all day and make the house smell good. Maybe she'll bake cookies and let us lick the bowls." I said this to Jared well into hour-two of driving. He wiggled in his seat to get comfortable, tapped his fingers rapidly on the steering wheel, gave a deep sigh and said how stupid it was to be following someone's grandmother to the center of the Earth. I hated that we had to do this too, but I felt worse for Jared. This person wasn't his grandma. As close as we were, I still didn't know everything about his family. He never talked about it, unless I thought to ask.

"So, where's your grandma? Do you talk to her?"

"No, my dad's mom died when I was little, don't remember if I ever met her. I met my mom's mother, but she died when I was about five, two years before my mom got sick and died. Sure hope your grandma is healthy. I have bad luck keeping the women in my life around. I'm a curse."

How could he call himself that? "You're not bad luck, Jared, okay? You're the only thing good in my life lately."

"Maybe you haven't been around me long enough. Or, maybe you don't see that your mom's arrest is partly my dad's fault, so I am a curse because he and I walked into your life and ruined it. He's such a jerk. Doesn't he give a damn about anyone but himself?" The veins on Jared's neck bulged, his face turned red.

"Jared, stop. You're not a curse. Your dad? Probably. We need to find him."

He shook his head. "Em, we'd find nothing but trouble and I don't think we want to get involved. Honestly, the fact that he's disappeared is probably good."

"Good? How can it be good? He shouldn't be running free while my mom is in jail. He has to know something. He's gotta be involved. It isn't fair."

Jared slammed on the breaks, swerved the car to the side of the road.

"I can't drive and talk about this," he said as he blinked back tears, laid his forehead on the steering wheel.

"Hey, Jared, maybe we should get out, get some fresh air or something." I felt bad that I had made him upset.

He lifted his head, his face wet with tears. "I found three thousand dollars in an empty ice cream tub in the freezer once when I was six. I thought I'd won some contest sponsored by the ice cream company. I jumped up and down, yelled, 'Whoa! Dad! Look what we won!' He ran in, yanked the cash out of my hand, said, 'Give me that and keep quiet. Don't tell anyone you found this.'"

He turned and looked at me the way I imagined he would have looked at his dad, with eyes wide, angry. "Don't tell anyone? Why? That's what I wanted to know. I thought of all the things we could do with that money. Go on a vacation, get Mom away for a while or find her a doctor who could cure her cancer rather than wait for her to die."

"Yeah," I said shocked, "how could he expect you to keep quiet? How does he not explain three thousand dollars in an ice cream tub?" The car shook as a semi-trailer passed us on the highway.

"And when I was eight, only a year after my mom died, he left for five days without telling me. Who does that to a kid who just lost his mom? What the heck is wrong with him?"

"That is so messed up. I can't believe he would do that. Well, it's Richard, so maybe I can."

I stared out the window at the brown hills that looked thirsty, needing rain. Cows slept on the ground or pulled weedy grass into their mouths.

"Our housekeeper, Isabella, woke me up when she came in my room to clean, asked why I wasn't in school, checked my temperature and told me I didn't have a fever. I had meant to wake up, thought I set my alarm, but it didn't go off." Jared paused, glanced out the window, swiped his hand through his hair. "I asked Isabella if my dad was there, and she said she hadn't seen him, so I jumped out of bed to get ready, sort of freaking out that I'd be over an hour late. Isabella didn't drive, so she walked with me to school, gave me her lunch when we got there, and told me not to worry when the lady in the school office glared at me while giving me an unexcused tardy slip."

"Weren't you scared to death? What did you do for five days by yourself?"

"Yeah, I was scared. I didn't know what to do. Isabella brought her husband and kids over, cooked for me, stayed in sleeping bags on the living room floor. She had watched me before when Mom was sick and Dad had to travel. She said he probably forgot to tell us he had travel plans, said it was no big deal. But when he walked in the door on that fifth day, man, she let him have it."

"Well, I would hope so. What did she say?"

"She yelled a bunch of stuff in Spanish I couldn't understand. I don't think he understood either, but he knew she was furious. He handed her a wad of cash and apologized. Her eyes lit up, she gave my dad a big hug. 'Gracias, gracias,' she said over and over. Must have been a lot of money to change quickly from angry mama bear to grateful, submissive servant. I didn't want her to leave. I felt like I was saying goodbye to my mom again. I liked the way she made hot meals for me, and even the way she made me clean my room and do my homework. I didn't want to be alone anymore, which is what I was with my dad."

"Did he say sorry to you? Give you a reason why he took off?"

"Not really. Handed me a hundred dollar bill, told me to stop looking at him with those big sad eyes. So I did. Went to my room and stared at that hundred dollar bill, wondered how many more I needed to get away from him, be on my own, or beg Isabella to let me live with her."

Jared's story made my life look like a dream. "I always thought I wanted to meet my dad," I said, "but maybe it's better not to have one."

"Yeah, I wish my dad would have left before I was born like your dad did. I think that'd be easier. I'm sick of life with him. If it weren't for you, I'd be outta here. Take my hundred dollar bills he's given me and live on my own."

Then it hit me. Jared was all I had left. "You could leave, especially if you have enough money to make it on your own," I said this as sincerely as I could even though I didn't mean it. Maybe I needed to hear from him that he cared about me enough to stay.

"No, Em, I won't be like him. I won't leave. If I can put up with him, I can put up with your grandma for the little bit we'll be here."

I could feel the heat of panic begin to rise. "What do you

mean, 'for the little bit we'll be here?' You don't think it will be for more than a couple days, do you?" This had to be temporary. My mom would post bail and be out.

Jared shrugged. "I don't think so, but nobody's told us anything. I'm just saying, whatever happens, we're in this together, okay?"

"Together." I smiled at that word that meant more to me now than ever. I knew I couldn't handle all this alone.

I dozed off after that, dreamed of eight-year-old Jared who'd been left alone with his housekeeper's family, glared at by the stupid attendance lady, brushed off by the filthy green money Richard selfishly obtained. Then I saw that money swirling around Jared, a tornado of hundred dollar bills lifting him away from the truck, away from me. I awoke to the sound of tires driving along a gravely road, saw the long dirt driveway that had to be grandma's, felt something clenched between my hands. "What's this?" I asked and opened my hand to see a wad of hundred dollar bills.

Jared smiled, his eyes steady on the driveway as he pulled to a stop and said, "Proof that I'm not leaving. Keep it."

# 4

Grandma's house sat between barren hills, a few oak and pine trees, and patches of wild lupine and poppies. Once inside, I felt relieved that we hadn't brought more stuff. Her shoebox of a home was filled to the brim with what I could best describe as outdoorsy clutter. She didn't have space for much more of anything.

Along the walls hung rows of dried flowers and sticks arranged into unique patterns and shapes. Rocks and leaves covered the table. Bowls and vases held seashells, twigs, flower petals, or pebbles sorted by different colors, sizes, shapes. I smelled wet dirt, caught an occasional whiff of lavender, and picked up a leafy plant with the aroma of pasta sauce. Basil was what Grandma called it. I was sure Grandma was a mad scientist, but not the kind who mixed potions and chemicals.

"Jared and Emily, welcome to your new home for a while," she said. "I know it's tiny, and probably a bit different than what you're used to, but I hope you'll feel comfortable here." She reached her hand into her purse, pulled out the leaf and twig I'd seen her take back at our house. She placed them in their proper bowls on the table, then lifted one of the bowls and held it in front of her eyes.

"Aha, there it is. Let me tell you the story about this." She plucked a tiny brown twig from the bowl. "This stick, such a precious, lovely thing." Grandma brought it right to her eye, kissed it. "Shall I tell them the story about you?"

Grandma talked to sticks, great.

"You remember the story, don't you?" She lifted a brow at the stick, winked at it. "Come sit down over here, I'll tell you."

I didn't budge. I wanted to know how long she thought we'd be staying. And was she talking to us or the stick?

She shuffled to the small wooden dining table with the stick held carefully between two fingers, stopped when she met the table, lifted the stick high above her head like an item to sacrifice. She hummed a tune, uttering words too quiet to understand, other than the occasional Jesus and Lord. Finally, she placed the stick in the center of the table and stared at it like a mama, proud of her newborn baby.

She snapped out of her worshipful moment when she saw we hadn't followed. "Come on, you two." She waved us over. "Didn't I say to come sit?"

Jared led, we sat down, Grandma began. I waited for her to somehow connect the stick to a way to get my mom out of jail, or to a way to get us back home soon. "Well, one day I was walking to the grocery store, noticing every little thing on the ground that was so boring, and I thought to myself that nothing God makes can be boring. Nothing. So, I picked up this stick, and then . . ."

I stopped listening. While she rambled, my mind begged her to shut up. Jared tapped his fingers on the table. I tried to figure out what angry song played in his mind to match the rhythm.

The cell phone in my hands vibrated, flashed my best friend Brit's name with a text message that said, *Hey, police are at your house, and you weren't at school today. What's going on? Are you okay?* I pictured her face with its lightly freckled nose and rosy cheeks, her auburn hair pulled back into a messy ponytail to reveal her forehead wrinkled with worry. I started to text *Yes, I'm fine* out of habit, but then I deleted it. That wasn't true. I wasn't fine. But how could I explain all this to her in a text? And I didn't want to talk to anyone about any of this. I didn't want to admit that my mom had been arrested and hear sympathetic words that would later turn into gossip I couldn't deny or defend.

"Emily? Jared?" Grandma said. Her head leaned closer to us, eyes wide. She must have asked us a question, but I had no idea what. Jared's bewildered stare told me he had no idea either.

"Aww, come on now. It's not a trick question." Grandma waited again for an answer to the question we didn't hear. "You two weren't listening, were you?" She pushed herself away from the table, stood up, snatched the stick and held it tight to her chest. "I'm sorry. I should know better. Stories make me feel better, but sometimes I need to just be quiet."

I felt bad now. I knew how it felt to be unheard.

"I just want to know what's going on," Jared said. "The police didn't tell us anything other than Tiffany was arrested on drug charges and that we were to stay with you. And nothing personal, but I kind of want to know why we can't just stay with friends for a couple days. This is a long way from home. We've got school, sports, friends. None of this makes any sense."

Grandma took a deep breath, let it out. "Well, I can tell you what the police told me." She glanced down at the stick, still clutched close to her. I hoped she wouldn't start storytelling again. "The police officer asked me if I could keep you indefinitely. You need to be with a legal guardian. They said the investigation and trial could take awhile."

"What does awhile mean?" I felt like I couldn't breathe.

"The lady officer said all this could take several months or more."

*Months?* I needed to run. My heart raced, my eyes filled

with tears, my throat wanted to scream but nothing came out. I was drowning in air, in the tight space that filled this twig-, stone-, leaf-filled room. I jumped up, bolted out the door, sprinted in the direction we'd come.

How were Jared and I going to continue school? Was I supposed to start up somewhere new, leave my mother, all my friends, forget about the tests and projects I had due in the next week? What about my articles I'd written for the yearbook? What about track season starting in a month? What about Jared's spot on the basketball team?

My feet, in old, worn-out Vans, pounded hard on the dusty dirt drive. My ankle, the one that kept me from competing in track, throbbed, yelled at me to stop. I ran harder. Mom's face flashed in my mind, her tears, handcuffs, all the things I left at home because I thought we'd be back. My toe hit a rock, I jolted forward, flew through the air, crashed, face and hands down. I lay there and cried, my forehead and nose throbbing, not wanting to move. The dirt stuck to my tears.

"Emily, hey," I felt two hands roll me over. Jared brushed my hair out of my eyes, rubbed the sleeve of his sweatshirt under my eyes. "Come on, Em. Don't run off like that, okay?"

He lifted my head in his arms, hugged me, rubbed my head the way Mom used to when we were sick or couldn't sleep. I felt his heart pounding, his chest heaving up and down. "Aside from scarin' me to death, you're way too fast. Shouldn't you run slower with a hurt ankle?"

"I'm sorry, I couldn't sit in there. I had to leave. My ankle's killing me, and that stupid boulder tripped me." I pointed to the shiny, dark stone on the path.

"I'd hardly call that a boulder," Jared said.

"I know, but it felt like one when I tripped on it." I reached for my ankle that throbbed like it did when I injured it at track practice a couple months earlier. I hadn't run much since then and had forgotten about it until now. Jared stretched his arm out, grabbed the rock that had taken me out. I watched it glisten in the sun.

"It's pretty cool actually," he said.

"Quiet, don't let Grandma hear you say that. She'll tell us a story about it."

"Hey, are you okay?" I looked up to see a large girl about our age, more out of breath than us. She held a water bottle in one hand, a cell phone in another. She pulled out an earphone from one ear. I heard a familiar rap beat.

"I saw you two running from Crazy Carol's house. Did she scare you or something? You two must be new. I haven't seen you around here before." She wiped sweat from her forehead with the hem of her neon-orange T-shirt. Her confidence to wear that color along with skin tight shorts at least three sizes too small impressed me.

"Crazy Carol?" I said.

"Yeah, the lady that lives there. You're definitely not from around here if you don't know about her. She walks around with bags of stuff she collects—leaves, weeds, rocks, probably bugs and snakes too for all I know. Sometimes she talks out loud to them, sort of creeps me out. I sometimes tell myself she's chasing me with a stick when I run this direction, helps me move quicker when I'd rather stop, walk home, eat ice cream. I gotta fit into a decent prom dress somehow. I'm only a sophomore, but my friend Chris is a junior, and he invited me. So, I don't want to look like a beast."

I brushed the dirt off my hands. It smeared and stuck in the bloody scratches that stung my palms.

"Enough of me. You look pretty banged up. Can I get you a ride home or something?"

"Yeah, I wish," I said.

"Oh, it's no problem. I live real close. I can't drive you, at least not legally. I'm still one horribly long year away from sweet sixteen, but I can ask my mom. She won't mind, really."

"No, no, I didn't mean that. I'm really okay. I don't need a ride." I was definitely not going to tell her Crazy Carol was my Grandma. If she knew that, who knows what I'd be called around this town. I pushed myself up from the dirt. Jared helped me, kept his hands close like I was a tower of children's blocks that might tumble down any second. "So, I get why people might think it's weird to collect all that stuff, but is that lady actually crazy?" Maybe Ginny knew something we should know.

She shrugged. "Heck, I don't know. Not much happens around here. We gotta come up with something to talk about. Most of us have nicknames of some sort. There's Jerry down the street, known as Watchtower, cause he stands in his open garage or front yard all day and night, always knows what's going on. There's Janine, lives the other direction, we call her Mrs. Fields cause she's always baking cookies for the kids in the neighborhood. She's not a good one to run by, makes you think too much about sitting and devouring one of those cookies. And me, I'm Giant Ginny, that name used to make me mad, now I just deal with it." She smiled, but her eyes looked sad, or tough, or both.

"Well, I'm Emily. This is Jared."

Jared reached out a hand toward her, "Nice to meet you, Ginny."

She shook his hand, blushed like most girls did when they met him, like I'm sure I did. "So you guys still haven't told me where you're from. Are you visiting? Just moved in? I guess I've been talking too much for you to answer that."

"Oh, yep, we're new," Jared said. "That Crazy Carol is Emily's grandma."

Jared and I trudged back to Grandma's after Ginny left.

"What on earth made you think it was a good idea to tell Ginny that the crazy person she described was my Grandma?" I shoved Jared in the shoulder and stopped walking.

He stopped, rubbed his hand through his hair like he always did when he was nervous, stared at the ground for a bit. "Yeah, sorry about that. I wasn't thinking about how that might make you feel. I was more interested in seeing her reaction. You have to admit, it was kind of funny."

I pictured Ginny's wide eyes with her hands over her mouth, completely dumbfounded as to what to say next. I let out a laugh. He was right. It was funny. "I think she apologized at least twenty times for calling my grandma crazy. But she seems pretty cool, right?"

Jared nodded and smiled. We told her it didn't matter, that we got it, completely. She pointed to the street where she lived, told us her phone number which I put in my phone. I liked Ginny's blunt honesty. I figured she'd tell me if I had spinach between my teeth or a bad hair day, but would also not care if I let my teeth and hair stay that way. Since we were apparently going to be staying awhile, at least I had met one person I could tolerate.

My feet felt heavy in the dry grass that nearly reached my knees. The crunching sound of each step made me think of all the things I wanted to stomp out of my life. I stomped the police first—the ones who said Mom was a drug trafficker. That was so ridiculous. I remembered talking to her about drugs when I took high school health class. I read aloud to my mom the list of nicknames for all the different drugs kids try. As a nurse, she knew what all those drugs did, but was surprised by how much I knew. She took notes, got on the phone with one of her friends.

"Can you believe all the names they have for this stuff and all the stupid things kids try these days?" she said. Then Mom got on a mission to save every teenage soul any way she could. She set up meetings with the school counselors, the school police, the PTA. Finally, she started a program called Safe House. She gathered names of parents who promised to keep a drug free home. If a kid wanted to hang out at someone's house, the parents could check the list on the school website, see if the house was drug free. The only problem was, most parents forgot or didn't bother to turn in the form, so there weren't that many safe houses. But she published what she had anyway, determined to go knock on doors to get more homes signed up.

Richard stopped that.

"That's a waste of your time. No one cares. All those parents you didn't hear from either allow their kids to inhale, or pop a pill, or use themselves. Can you get me more coffee while you're up?" he said one morning after breakfast.

Mom's expression went from school spirit leader to sad clown in the ten seconds Richard took to squelch her dream of teen savior. Why didn't she tell him to shut up and get his own coffee? Something about him kept her from speaking her mind, and it made me crazy. Richard had that same effect on Jared.

I first met Jared in my seventh grade P.E. class. His teacher was absent and there was no substitute teacher, so my teacher,

Mrs. Mancher, combined her eighth grade class with our seventh grade class. What I'd describe as mayhem with one class became World War III with two classes. Some kids chased each other around on the basketball courts, some obediently huddled around the sidelines to wait for Mrs. Mancher's instruction. One kid skipped around with his sweatshirt covering his eyes and ran into a basketball pole. Two of his friends helped him to the office for ice.

"Some of you go run laps on the field. Some of you stay and cheer on the basketball players," Mrs. Mancher said. Class control was clearly not her strength. Who would choose laps? Only Sam, who won the jog-a-thon every year, sprinted away with fierce determination as if someone might challenge him. I didn't know how I got so lucky, but Mrs. Mancher's wisdom chose me as point guard on Jared's team. I played basketball at about the same level as kindergartners, which was why I decided to run track. It didn't require a ball in my hand.

I ran down the court, dribbled the ball with loud swats of my palm, not with my fingertips the way Mrs. Mancher taught us. *Don't travel, don't trip, focus,* I repeated in my head. When I reached the other end of the court, I stopped, saw Jared near the basket.

"Here! Pass!" he yelled. I launched the ball and hit some eighth grade boy on his head.

"I'm so sorry!" I yelled.

"What the heck is your problem?" the boy yelled back. He grabbed the ball from the ground, chucked it at my face. It hit me with a loud smack. I covered my throbbing eye with one hand, tried not to cry, but couldn't hold it in. With my good eye, I saw Jared grab the boy's shirt, throw him onto the ground and yell, "What's your problem, idiot?"

The boy hit the ground as violently as that ball hit my eye. He rolled back and forth, moaned, held the back of his head. Of course the highly qualified and observant Mrs. Mancher finally noticed and ran to the scene. She sent Jared to the office without hearing the whole story. Even when I tried to explain, she didn't change her mind. The principal suspended him for two days.

The day Jared came back from suspension, I saw him on the soccer field at P.E. We weren't supposed to talk to kids in other classes, but I didn't care. When we ran laps, I sidled over to him.

"Hey, I'm sorry about what happened. Thanks for sticking up for me though," I said.

"I'd do it again. No big deal. That guy's a loser. He'll get his payback someday." That was when I saw the huge welt under his eye. His looked a lot worse than my eye felt when that ball hit me.

"Hey, are you okay? Your eye looks horrible."

"Yeah, I'm fine. Just had a little accident, no big deal."

I wanted to ask what kind of accident, but he looked down and away from me, then said, "Okay, uhh, see you later," and ran ahead. He clearly didn't want to talk about it.

Jared lived a street away from me, so we walked home together that day. He never said any more about the eye, but when we got to his house a block before mine, Richard drove past. He slowed his car, rolled down the window. "Hey, think you could walk any slower? Thought you'd be home by now. I got called in to work. Didn't have time to get stuff for dinner. Should be something in that fridge though. Who's your friend?"

"Emily, she's the girl in the P.E. class I tried to tell you about."

Richard rolled his eyes. "Oh yeah, the one who got you suspended."

Jared shook his head, "She didn't get me suspended. That's not what I told you. I said she was . . ."

"Yeah, yeah Prince Charming," Richard said, "I get it. Nice to meet you, Emily." Richard drove off, but his chill stayed in the air.

# —6—

A cool breeze sent a shiver through me at the same moment I thought about Richard. Jared and I sat in the dirt in front of Grandma's house, not quite the same as the spongy lawn we had sat on earlier at home. The sky turned a purple orange hue, the same sunset we had at home at least. Mom used to comment on the sunset a lot as she made dinner and gazed out the kitchen window. "I know you don't want to get in touch with your dad," I said to Jared, "but I've gotta talk to my mom. I can't just sit around here doing nothing when we could maybe do something to help. Can you take me to see her?"

He looked at me with those crystal-blue eyes that seemed to look right inside my heart, like he totally got me. "Yeah, I can take you to see her. Do you think you can handle that? Seeing your mom in jail?"

"Do I have a choice? Not seeing her at all is worse."

Jared stopped, looked up at the sky, his eyes clouded over. He pressed his fingers against his lids and turned away from me.

"Jared, you okay?" I asked. I'd never seen him cry before, but I felt pretty sure that's what he was trying to hide.

"I'm sorry about my dad," he said, "If he's the reason your mom's in jail, I'm really sorry."

"Jared, it's not your fault. You're here for me, just like you said you would be. I don't blame you for any of this, okay?" I reached for his shoulder. He turned and I saw his face, fresh tears rolling down his cheeks as soon as he wiped one away. I reached around him with both arms and hugged him close. His shirt smelled of the lavender detergent Mom used. His arms squeezed tight around me, like he didn't want to let go.

The front door of Grandma's house swung open wide. Grandma bustled out of it and down her front steps. "Oh, I'm so glad you're back. I thought maybe you started running all the way home. You were outta here so fast, and gone so far I couldn't see you. I finally found my keys and was coming to look for you." She held her hands to her chest, breathing about as hard as I did after a race. "How about we all go inside? I'll make you something to eat."

I thought maybe I should apologize for taking off, but I didn't feel like saying sorry to anyone. I felt like everyone except Jared should be saying sorry to me. We continued to plod through the dry weeds to Grandma's front porch. Grandma picked up something from the ground on the way in. I wondered how she could possibly find any more items to collect when they all seemed to be gathered inside her house.

"So, how about I show you your rooms?" Grandma said. "Then I'll get dinner going. I made some soup from the tomatoes in my garden yesterday, thought I'd heat some of that up. And you both like grilled cheese, don't you? Seems kids always like that."

"Yeah, that sounds good," Jared said. I nodded in agreement and tried to smile as politely as Jared did.

We walked down a short narrow hallway. On the right was a bedroom with a puffy queen-size bed covered in multicolored quilts and pillows. I hoped that was my room.

"So that's my room on the right," Grandma said, killing my wish for that room.

The room to the left had a twin bed, a dark blue comforter spread across it, and a single pillow with a stuffed bear propped on it. As we entered this room, I noticed stacks of boxes from floor to ceiling lined up in front of a small closet.

"Jared, I hope this is okay for you. The bed is a bit small for you I think, but it's what I've got for now, and I apologize for all the boxes. This room's been my place to store all my keepsakes and collections. The closet's jam-packed too. I'll find a better place for everything, but for now this dresser has some empty drawers.

Jared looked like a shocked giant in a tiny elf room, but he still managed to pull off a smile and a polite comment. "It's fine. Don't worry about it. I don't have that much stuff."

I wasn't sure how he thought all the things he loaded into the truck earlier wasn't much stuff, but maybe he planned to bring only some of it inside.

"Emily, I thought you could have your mom's old room. It doesn't look much different than how she left it. Keeping it the same made me feel like a piece of her was still here. Maybe that'll help you in all this too."

The idea sounded nice, but when I entered, the ghostly presence of my mom made me miss her more. The bed was covered in a pale yellow comforter with pillows that had tulips embroidered on them. I picked one up and ran my hand along it.

"Your mom made those," Grandma said. "She liked to sew. She sometimes sewed her own clothes for school, always felt proud to have something no one else could find in the stores."

I forced a smile, and set the pillow down. White shelves were filled with books, small glass animals, a rag doll, a basket of old magazines. A desk was in the corner with a pedestal mirror on top, a pencil holder, and a framed picture of my younger mom and a boy. I picked it up and admired her smile, her hair, beautiful even in an outdated style. She wore a long, narrow black gown, strapless, and had a corsage around her wrist. The boy next to her was tall, dark hair, big smile, handsome.

"Who's in the picture with her?" I asked.

"Oh, um," Grandma paused and looked sad. "That's Landon Sharpe, your father, Emily."

Now I truly felt overwhelmed. My imprisoned mother and my father who I never met in the same room, smiling at me behind a glass frame. They felt all too close and all too far away at the same time.

I knew she wanted a positive response to staying in this room, but I wasn't sure how to dredge one up.

I thought of Mom, in a jail cell, and realized I could be in a worse spot. "All right, thanks." I said.

Grandma smiled, straightened out the bedspread, waited for a second as if she wanted to help. But then she smiled and said, "Okay, you two can grab your things out of Jared's truck and unpack while I fix dinner."

I plopped onto the bed, looked up at Jared, the only thing I could look at now and not cry.

"You okay? You want to go get our stuff?" Jared asked.

"Yeah, in a minute," I said. I laid my head down on the pillow, stared around at the room, realized how exhausted I was.

"I can get your suitcase. You stay here, figure out how to make my room bigger or something." I thanked him. He had to be tired too, but he still acted like a gentleman. No wonder so many girls had a crush on him.

I rolled over and noticed a box on the floor, labeled Tiffany. I opened the lid. Two Barbie dolls and a pink stuffed poodle rested on top. I pulled them out, imagining Mom as a little girl with her prized possessions. Beneath these I found stacks of paper and journals. I could see who I got my journal fetish from. Picking one out of the box, I rubbed the cover, opened it to the first page. It was dated June 5, 1996. I knew Mom was thirty-five now, born in 1984, so this was from when she was twelve. I began to read the swirly round cursive that filled the page. I was thankful for my third grade teacher who insisted that someday we would need to read or write something in cursive, in spite of how little I or anyone I knew actually used it since then.

*Dear Diary,*

*Mom and Dad say we have to move. I am so mad! Dad promised that we would stop moving around, that this last move was our final one. But, he lied. Mom bought me this diary, said I could fill it up with the events of our adventure to California. I know she was trying to make it sound fun even though she isn't happy about it either. She says that's what happens when you're a military family. But I wish we could stay put and he could just go. He's always drinking at home and yelling at Mom. I can't wait until I can be a grown up. Then I'll move away because I want to, not because I have to.*

Jared returned, his guitar strap around his neck, his guitar swaying back and forth as he dropped his suitcase from one hand, mine from the other, and then pushed my box of journals into the room with one foot. "I think I got everything," he said. He loved the challenge of carrying everything in from the car at once. My mom enjoyed shopping a lot more once Richard and Jared moved in with us because Jared always carried all the groceries in; about six plastic bags lined up on each arm, his hands grasping one or two more. It was quite a feat, and a little weird, I thought, that he actually wanted to do that. But then I saw how little he cleaned up his laundry and realized where the saved energy came from.

"What are you reading?" he asked. I suddenly felt guilty, like I was reading something I shouldn't. I knew how private my journal was. But Jared wouldn't care, and if Mom didn't want them read, she shouldn't have left them with her mom.

"My mom's journal, it was in the closet, along with tons more. I won't be bored now," I said.

"Wow, that's cool. Your mom wrote just like you."

I felt proud whenever someone pointed out something about me that was like my mom, like the green color of our eyes, or the way we both smiled. That's why I knew it was wrong for her to be in jail. That couldn't be who she was, a criminal. She had to be innocent. When I saw her, I would figure out how to prove it.

# —7—

The last time I had soup it came from a can. Recently, Mom worked weird hours on her nursing shift and slept a lot when she was at home, so I had learned to grab whatever was available and easy to make. I wasn't sure what made Grandma's tomato soup so much better. I figured a tomato is a tomato, can't really improve upon it. So, Campbell's tomato soup was what I thought I would taste when I spooned her soup into my mouth. Wrong! It was a perfect combination of sweet and spicy and tangy. Grandma went on about how it was made with fresh homegrown tomatoes, which were always sweeter and tastier than what could be bought at the store, plus fresh oregano, basil, garlic and lemon, stewed slowly to bring out all the flavors. The grilled cheese sandwich was made on thickly cut homemade bread, and a plate of chocolate brownies topped off the meal. But in spite of how great it tasted, I still longed for canned soup with Mom. I felt like I shouldn't enjoy Grandma's food. If Mom didn't get along with Grandma, it was for a reason. There had to be something I shouldn't trust.

"So, I won't share any stories with you, unless you want me to," Grandma said before she bit into a brownie. She dipped her tea bag up and down in her cup. Then she picked up the string end and read the tea tag attached to it. "But you might enjoy hearing this: 'Love is at the root of all good things,' it says. I do believe that to be true," she said. She picked up a pair of tiny scissors, the kind I'd seen my mom use to cut thread to sew a button or hem a pair of pants. Grandma snipped the tea bag string, then lifted the lid from a blue and white speckled bowl that sat on the table and tossed the string inside.

"Do you get money for those or something?" Jared asked, reminding me of all the cereal box tops I saved that earned money for the school.

"Oh, no, I don't save them for any money. I just like what they have to say. There's real power in words, ya know. So, when I need some power, the words are as close as this bowl, or as near as the good book, the Bible, that is. That's got a lot of powerful words in it."

It scared me a little to realize I had something in common with Grandma, the lady known about town to be crazy. All those quotes I collected in my journals were sort of like the tea bag quotes Grandma collected in that bowl. And actually, all those stuffed animals I saved and never wanted to give away, each one with a story I could tell about why it was so special, were sort of like Grandma's sticks, leaves, flower petals, and pebbles.

Grandma must have seen the fear in my face. "You okay Emily dear?" she asked. "You can be excused any time. You both must be tired. Tomorrow you sleep as long as you want. There's no need to get up and do anything. Just rest."

Maybe Grandma thought the idea of sleeping in would put us at ease, but I felt my heart beat faster at the thought. "I wish I felt good about that. I have a Spanish quiz every Friday, worth ten percent of my grade, and I'm missing that tomorrow. I also have a paper due in English, and tests next week. I'm not going to get the track scholarship I need with my race times alone. I need to have good grades too."

"I understand. Perhaps we can go down to the school here

in town, Pine View High, and look to see about getting you enrolled. We don't want you two falling behind. This all happened so suddenly—"

"Actually, we're planning to go visit Tiffany," Jared interrupted. "Do you want to come with us?"

And now there was that reminder, the gut-wrenching truth that I was going to jail tomorrow instead of school. It was all too much.

"Oh, well, uh, no, I don't think so," She waved her hand at us like she was shooing the idea away. "I think she would rather just see you two. I can look into the school enrollment while you're gone." She popped up from her seat, took the lid back off the tea bag quote bowl, grabbed a handful of tea bag stems, and walked into the living room.

"Let your inner light shine; it is only you who holds the key to your own happiness; the more you love the less you need; we live in the . . ." Grandma's voice continued, reading off teabag quotes, but I could no longer hear her as she walked down the hallway.

"Of course she doesn't want to go," I whispered to Jared. "She doesn't like her own daughter. She's probably thinking she is rescuing us from her or something. I can't wait to talk to Mom and find out how much longer we need to be here."

"She must like her if she's willing to take us in, Em" Jared said. "And she said your mom's room was the same because it made her feel like she was still here. Just because they don't get along doesn't mean they don't care about each other."

Jared spoke like he knew how that felt. Maybe he was thinking about himself and his dad when he said that. But I didn't know how he could care about his dad after all he had done wrong. A chilly breeze blew through the open window behind me, and I pulled my sleeves down over my hands. Grandma walked back in with a sweater over her shoulders, holding a big thick book. She switched on the light that hung over the table, sat down in the chair next to me, and set the book down. I saw that it was the Bible. I hoped she wasn't going to start reading to us. She opened it, flipped the pages, and remained on one page. She hummed something while she read, but didn't read anything aloud. I wondered if the Bible was making her think badly of Mom, making her think she must have done something horrible to be arrested and put in jail. Maybe she heard God telling her to stay away from Mom, and to steer us away from her too.

"So, why don't you think Mom would want to see you tomorrow?" I asked. She kept reading and humming, completely in a zone of some sort. I waited a few more seconds and then said, "Grandma?"

She popped out of her zone, "Oh, yes?"

"Why don't you want to go with us tomorrow? Why do you think Mom wouldn't want to see you?"

"Well, dear, your mom and I haven't exactly spoken much in the past year. We had a little argument over the phone that didn't end so well and I haven't talked to her since. The phone call from the police was a bit of a surprise. I wouldn't have expected her to leave you with me when she was in trouble, but I guess I'm all she's got."

"I remember that phone call. Mom was really upset. She made it sound like the argument was your fault, like she tried to be nice but you wouldn't listen."

Grandma laughed, looked down at the Bible, appeared to read a bit of it and then said, "Sometimes people think you aren't listening when you don't agree with them. I was listening to your mom, listening real well, but I didn't agree with her, and she didn't like that."

"She said *you* wouldn't speak to *her*," I replied. I was breathing faster, trying not to yell, though I could hear my voice rising. She said you never called her back after she tried to get in touch with you."

Again, Grandma laughed, but it wasn't a real one. It was more the type of laugh I gave when someone annoyed me and I said "whatever," and rolled my eyes.

"I know better than to hunt your mother down when she's angry. It usually doesn't work. She did the same thing when she was your age, got mad about stuff and then stopped talking to me, or took off and came back hours later after I was worried sick and searched all over town for her. In fact, that's how she met your father, went for a run after an argument with me and met him on the same path. You know that story?"

"No, my mom doesn't like to talk about my dad. I only know he doesn't want anything to do with me."

Grandma's eyes opened wide, "Really? Well, I wouldn't be so sure about that. He might want something to do with you, but hasn't had a chance to tell you."

"I'm fifteen. How much time does he need?" I said. "And why would you think he hasn't had a chance? It can't be that hard to find me."

Grandma stared at me, like she wanted to say something again but didn't. "I don't mean to upset you, Emily. We can talk about your father another day. I promised you no more stories tonight."

Part of me wanted to hear her story, to hear what she knew about my father. But the other side of me felt she would tell me a lie, or a side of the story that made my mom look bad. I couldn't take hearing another bad thing about her. I left the table, didn't clear my bowl or plate, didn't thank Grandma for dinner. I went to my bedroom, which felt more like a museum exhibit of my mom's childhood, and fell onto the bed.

I looked at my phone, flipped through my Instagram feed, but that only reminded me of my friends, home, everything I had lost in the past twenty-four hours. I still didn't know what to do about school. Should I just have Grandma call me in absent? How long would that be? Would I be excused? Did I really want to enroll at Pine View? It was all so overwhelming. I put my phone down and felt Mom's old journal at my fingertips. I picked it up, opened the pages, and held them to my chest. My mom's words, close to my heart, helped me imagine she was near as I closed my eyes to sleep.

# 8

I awoke to the smell of bacon, the hard journal under my right cheek, Grandma singing, "This is the day, this is the day that the Lord has made, that the Lord has made." How could she sing so happy a tune? And if this is the day the Lord made, why is my mom in jail?

I remembered the dream I'd had about her that made me feel like I hadn't really slept at all. She was behind the ugly metal bars of a jail cell, lying on her small bed only three feet away from a rusty sink and a toilet. She shivered underneath a thin, white sheet. She cried, her chest heaved up and down, her tears soaked her pillow. A man in a guard's uniform appeared with keys, jangled them in front of her cell, smiled, said, "Hey girl, want these?"

My mom reached her hand out as she pushed herself up. "Yes, please," she whimpered. She stood slowly, an old woman, barely able to move, her hair gray like Grandma's, deep wrinkles across her face. In the dream, I stood there, behind the guard who teased my mom. I couldn't take it. I knocked the keys out of his hand, punched him in the gut. He bent forward and I kicked him in the head. He fell to the ground. I grabbed the keys from the floor. My hands shook as I tried to find the right one to fit the lock. I tried one, then another, and another.

None worked. I felt a hand around my ankle, the one I sprained in track. I tried to pull it away, then I felt my other ankle locked in the guard's grasp too.

"Let go! Leave me alone!" I had shouted as he looked up at me and laughed. Then I finally saw the guard's face, Richard.

I sat up quickly, told myself to forget that horrible dream. I saw my phone had six missed call alerts, all from Brit, along with a text message from Verizon Wireless saying phone service would be stopped within the next twenty-four hours if no payment was received. Wow, that was great news. As if losing my mom, my friends, and my school wasn't enough, now I'd have no way to even talk to them. The time on my phone showed 7:15. If I was going to school today, I'd be walking through the parking lot about now, looking for Brit so we could study for our Spanish quiz before first period started. Then we'd talk about what we were going to do tonight since it was a Friday. Jared would be next to me, probably not saying much as he didn't talk much in the morning. It usually took him a while to embrace the idea that he wasn't still in bed sleeping.

"I got up and walked barefoot across the cold wood floor to Jared's room. His feet hung over the edge of the bed, and his pillow was somehow on the floor in front of the door. I picked it up, tossed it gently at him. "Hey, time to wake up to your wonderful life."

I expected a simple pillow toss back, or a "No, let me sleep." Instead, I saw a Jared I hadn't seen before.

He jumped up, shouted, "Sorry, Mom, what's up? What do you need?" He looked around, saw me, then let out a deep breath. "Oh, Em, hey, I forgot where I was. Are you okay?"

"I'm fine. I didn't mean to startle you."

"Yeah, for a second there I thought I was with my mom."

Why would he think that? He clearly saw my confused look and continued, "When she was sick, I sometimes slept on the couch in her bedroom, told her to wake me if she needed anything. For a while, she wouldn't. She'd force herself up from bed to get water, or something to read, maybe another blanket. But eventually, she couldn't do it, and I wouldn't hear her call my name, probably because she could barely speak above a whisper at that time. Once she tossed this throw pillow she had on her bed to get my attention. That became my cue after that. The pillow touched me, I woke up, got her what she needed. Worked out pretty well. So, yeah, when that pillow hit me, I thought it was her. I guess I still forget she's not here sometimes."

"Sorry. I didn't mean to remind you of your mom that way."

"No, it's okay. That was a rough time, but at least she was here, we were together, a family. That part's good to remember."

Together, a family. He was right. That was important. At least Mom was alive. I could still see her, even if it was behind a jail cell window for a while. "Are you still okay with taking me to see my mom? She'll be glad to see you too."

"Of course, but first, take this." He threw the pillow back at me with about the same strength I saw him pass basketballs in a heated game.

"Hey! I laughed after it slammed my face. I lifted the pillow to swing at him, but he easily grabbed it.

"Ha! Nice try!" He ran out the doorway and into the bathroom, cracked the door open slightly and said, "I'll let you shower first, but only if you admit defeat."

I thought for a second, knowing he had pretty much won this battle with his grin and his smarts, two of his best weapons in any conflict. "Okay, fine," I said, "You win." If I didn't want to shower, or if he could just be ugly and irritating, I could have been more stubborn. He knew how to get to me.

He opened the door, one arm out straight to block me, the other clenching the pillow. He kept his eyes on me, smiled his winning grin.

"Go ahead, in you go." He motioned to the bathroom as he waited for me to pass.

I entered the bathroom and said, "Loser," then smiled my most winning smile and slammed the door before he could retaliate. I felt glad for those last few moments, running around, hassling each other. It was the first feeling of life the way it used to be.

After a quick shower, I threw on my jeans and faded blue track sweatshirt. Then I pulled my hair back into a braid so I wouldn't have to dry it. Today was a no makeup day, even though I never wore much. But to go to jail? I definitely didn't need to look pretty for that.

I entered the kitchen where Grandma still sang, picking petals off flowers and placing them in a bowl on the table. The strong scent of something sweet baking in the oven and the bacon sizzling made my tummy growl.

"Oh, good morning dear," she said. "I have breakfast ready if you'd like some before you go, and I packed you two some peanut butter and honey sandwiches and fresh oranges for the road."

She made it so difficult to hate her. If this was Mom's life growing up, I didn't understand why they didn't get along with each other. I could deal with obsessive nature collections in exchange for a hot breakfast and picnic lunches. I wanted to ask why she picked apart the flowers, but feared I'd hear a long story for each petal.

"I'll bet you think I'm crazy to tear flowers apart." She read my mind, which could have been proof that she was super smart, not crazy.

"Uhh, well, I am wondering about that a little," I admitted, dreading the earful I might get in response.

"These are dandelions and hibiscus, full of antioxidants. I steep them to make tea. Would you like to try some?"

"No, thanks, not today. Jared might though. He loves natural stuff."

"Oh, does he?" Her entire face lit up. Her eyes, the same

green as one of the flower stems in her hand, sparkled.

"Yep, total nature guy." Actually, he was the complete opposite, more a fast food and processed product kind of guy. But I knew he was too polite to turn away something she made and offered him, and I couldn't resist getting the last word in after losing the pillow battle.

"Well, he'll love this then. I'll make him some now so it's ready when he comes out."

Grandma carried the bowl of petals to the stove, placed them in a tea strainer, and poured water from the steaming kettle over them. Then she spooned honey into the cup and stirred as the petals steeped. Jared entered several minutes later to a place setting of homemade scones filled with blueberries and raspberries, hot bacon, and . . . the tea, which I told him he'd love. I smiled at him as he sipped and politely told Grandma how good it tasted.

When we pulled away in the truck after breakfast, Jared punched me in the upper arm, not hard enough to hurt, but enough to get my attention.

"Hey!" I said, rubbing my arm.

"That's for the gift of weed tea this morning. Thanks. It energized me so much I couldn't control my actions. My hand just swung right out there, couldn't help it."

I didn't hit him back. He and I both knew I had won. The shoulder punch didn't change that. I hoped the next battle I faced, seeing my mom in jail, would also be a win.

# 9

I think the most difficult part of the road trip was the stretch of highway where we passed our town. I could feel home as we neared it, not just see the familiar rolling hills dotted with houses, the Target shopping center, the ever-crowded In-N-Out Burger and the Chaparral Mall, but I could actually feel home—the comfort of my own bed, the familiarity of neighbors and friends, the ease I felt simply by being in a place where I could be myself. I even felt the same sense of excitement as when we traveled back from road trips to spots Mom loved, like San Francisco, San Diego, Las Vegas, ready to pull up to the driveway and plop on the couch, not a hotel bed. But I couldn't enjoy that feeling this time because there was no satisfying ending. I wasn't going home. I could feel Jared slow up for a second when we passed our normal exit, Birch Street. I looked over the rows and rows of houses, trees, winding streets, wished I could catch a small glimpse of my house. As my neck craned, I felt Jared speed up.

"Feels weird to keep going, doesn't it?" he said.

"Really weird," I said. I wanted to tell Jared to pull off the freeway, to go back to our house despite the fact that the police had secured it, saying the house would be under investigation for some time. I wanted to go inside, even for a little while, to soak in the feel of home again. But the more I thought about it, the more I realized it wouldn't feel like home anymore. It would feel disturbingly empty, almost haunted with the normalcy and memories that used to be there. So I stayed quiet, squelched that feeling of vomit about to pass into my throat.

I decided to finally call Brit. I missed her, and it wasn't fair to keep ignoring her calls and texts. Plus, if my phone service stopped while no one was paying for it, I'd regret not being able to talk to her whenever I wanted. I couldn't imagine sitting in Grandma's kitchen talking on a landline while she hummed Bible tunes in the background. After a few rings that felt like forever, I was relieved to hear that familiar, friendly voice.

"Emily? Thank God. I'm so glad to hear from you. I've been worried about you."

"I know, I'm sorry. A lot has happened. I really miss you."

"Hey, don't worry. I get it. So, what's going on? I heard your mom was arrested. I don't even know how that's possible. And where are you?"

I knew she would be shocked by the arrest, and I dreaded telling her everything. It forced me to believe it. "Yeah, it's true. How did you find out?" I paused, took a deep breath. "She was arrested on drug charges. Did you hear that?"

"What? No way, I hadn't heard about the drug charges. That girl who lives a couple doors down from you, Krystal, nearly tackled me in the school parking lot Thursday morning, said she saw the police at your house, but she didn't know what was going on. She thought maybe I knew something. That's why you have like a billion calls from me. Wow, Em, I don't even know what to say. Drug charges? I'm sorry, that doesn't seem like your mom's thing.

"Yeah, I know. I think she's innocent. I think Richard is behind all of it. I'm determined to find out."

"Oh yeah, Dick, our favorite guy."

That made me laugh. I loved when she referred to Richard

that way. She was actually the first one to tell me that traditional nickname for Richard. In his case it seemed fitting.

"He magically disappeared, and he isn't answering Jared's calls. I know he's behind this, Brit."

"Wow, unbelievable."

"I felt my heart racing at the thought of him. I pictured his unshaven face, his balding head, his smile that never really looked like a smile, more like an evil grin. He was probably sitting on a couch somewhere, watching television with a beer in his hand, while the rest of us dealt with the rubble of his tornado.

"So Jared and I are staying at my grandma's, like three hours away in the middle of nowhere."

I didn't want her to know I had just passed the exit to my house. She would have asked me to come over, and I knew I couldn't handle that. I couldn't face her parents, her brother and sister, tell them I was fine when I was actually a wreck.

"You have a grandma? Well, of course you do. Everyone does, but I didn't know you had one that was still alive or anything. You've never mentioned her."

"Yeah, well that's because my mom and her don't get along, so I haven't seen her since I was little. It's basically like living with a complete stranger."

"Wow, Em, I'm sorry. Is she nice?"

"Uh, yes, she's nice," I believed that so far, although nice wouldn't have been my first word to describe Grandma. "But she's kind of crazy."

"Oh, you mean crazy fun or actually crazy? Like she has a diagnosis of some mental illness? Or, is she a little different?"

Leave it to Brit to be literal. She hated when people used the wrong words to describe things. It was why I always had her read over my essays before turning them in. I was the creative, flowery writer. She was the exacting, scientific one."

"Well, I don't actually know for sure. She has all these

collections of rocks and leaves and dirt, and she talks about God way too much. Every minute is another Sunday School lesson that somehow connects to these random outdoor scraps. She was literally talking to sticks the other day, Brit. So, I call that crazy. In fact, so does everyone else. We found out from a girl we met that the whole town calls her Crazy Carol."

"Oh my, that's not good. But maybe she's not that bad. She must be okay if your mom trusted her to take care of you."

I had my doubts about Mom's judgment, but I didn't say that to Brit.

"Yeah, you're right. It could be worse I guess. We could be stuck with Richard."

"Anything's better than that. So, Jared's with you?"

"Yeah, he is," I said. I hoped she wouldn't say anything more about that with him right in the car next to me. She knew I'd had a bit of a crush on him, which had become awkward since he and Richard started living with us. I decided to thwart her possible teasing remarks. "He's right here, actually. Here Jared, say hi to Brit."

I moved the phone from my ear toward him. "Hi Brit!" he shouted, sounding remarkably cheerful even though I knew he didn't want to talk to anyone.

"Hey Jared! Hang in there, okay? I hope you guys can come back soon. I miss you guys!"

"Thanks, I hope we're back soon too."

I put the phone back to my ear. "Yeah, I don't know when we'll be back. My grandma said we could be here indefinitely, until my mom is out, so I don't know what that means, or what we're supposed to do about school. I can't imagine starting over here."

"What? Really? So, this isn't just a little visit with your grandma. You guys are actually moving in."

"I don't know, Brit. We haven't been told very much."

"Oh man, Em, this is all so crazy. If your ankle is feeling

better, you need to go for a good hard run. That always makes you feel better, right?"

I crossed my foot over my knee, rubbed my ankle. "Yeah, it was feeling better until I tripped over a rock in front of my grandma's house, so, we'll see. If I do stay here, I don't think I'll be trying out for the track team. I'd look like an idiot, horribly slow."

"You could probably hop on one foot and be fast enough," Brit said. "But if you're too hurt to run, that's a good reason."

"Yeah, well, you can run fast for me, okay?"

I didn't know if I actually meant that. The thought of no longer winning, no longer improving, made me feel empty.

"Okay, I'll try. But don't give up on that dream of yours. I mean, I'd love to beat the record before you, but you kept me motivated. It'll be weird racing without you to push me."

"Thanks Brit. I won't give up. Maybe I'll try running in the next couple days, see how I feel. The thought of you beating my time is killing me, no offense."

She laughed at this, as I knew she would. We were good enough friends to talk smack to each other about who was the better 800 meter runner, and who would prove it by beating the league record.

"So, can I do anything to help? You know you'd be welcome to live with me. My parents adore you. It really wouldn't be a problem."

"Thanks Brit. I would love that, but I don't think we have a choice right now, and I'm really trying to believe this is temporary, that we're going to prove my mom's innocence and this whole mess will go away."

"Okay, well don't be a stranger. I know you don't want to talk about this all the time. We can just talk about dumb things like always."

I laughed, thinking of all the stupid conversations we had about boys, the best running shoes, what college we'd go to, who we would marry, the best pizza toppings, how to annoy Richard. We could talk about everything and nothing that mattered in life.

"And I'm praying for you, Em. God's with you in all of this you know, not to sound like your grandma or anything."

I took words about God from Brit differently than from Grandma. Brit was the one who invited me to church for the first time, the one who prayed for me and helped me whenever I felt down about not seeing my dad, about how much I wished my mom wouldn't be with Richard. But even from her those words felt less comforting now than before.

"Yeah, thanks Brit."

"Do you want me to pray with you right now?"

I definitely didn't want that. "No, that's okay. I actually have to go. But I really appreciate it." It really did mean a lot that she was thinking about me, even if I wasn't sure her prayers would work.

"Okay, well, I'll talk to you soon. Hang in there, Em."

"Thanks again, Brit. Bye for now."

When I hung up, I felt relieved to have talked to her, but sad too. I wanted to go hang out at her house. I wanted to be able to laugh. I wanted to believe in those words she told me about God.

# –10–

An hour and a half later, we pulled off the freeway for the destination of all time, jail. The homesick feelings from before turned into fear. What would Mom look like in that jail uniform with a background of dull walls and hard cement floors? It seemed odd that a few flowers and shrubs were planted in front of the sign that read, "Women's Correctional Facility," as if they'd attempted to make the place look civilized. Beyond that lay pavement, barbed wire fences, and a looming building where I imagined hundreds of women caged. When Jared turned the engine off, I felt like my heart stopped too.

"I don't want to do this," I said.

"Hey, that's okay, Em. I can turn back around. I don't really like this place."

"No, I don't want to do it, but I have to. I have to see her and talk to her and find out how to get her out of this hellhole."

"All right, well, if anyone can do it, you can. You're a tough one, Emily Greene."

We entered the front building to be greeted by security officers. There were a lot more visitors than I expected. At least forty people waited in a line outside. I saw children younger than me, hands clenched to the hand of maybe a father, uncle, neighbor, cousin or aunt. Elderly people waited too, maybe to visit their adult children. I wondered what their story was, what happened to the person they visited today. It was the first time I felt like I wasn't alone in the world of imprisoned loved ones.

"Set any bags and electronic devices here to be scanned," an officer said.

I pulled my phone from my back pocket, and wondered why I felt like a criminal. Something about being in jail to visit a parent must have that effect, like you're guilty too even when you have nothing to do with the crime. We made it through the long line of people in security after full pat downs. Then we were escorted to a waiting room where we signed in.

Cold air blew through a vent above me. I folded my arms across my waist in hopes of blocking out the chill. I felt short of breath, like maybe I was having a panic attack even though I didn't know what that felt like. Glass windows separating the visitors from inmates quickly spoiled my hope of a hug. I searched the room for at least one colorful, cheery item. I found nothing, unless I counted the color red on the no smoking sign.

I thought maybe Mom could at least get a bright orange suit like prisoners wore on television shows. That might at least add some brightness to the gray walls and grumpy guard faces. But as a couple of inmates entered, I saw that plain white shirts with a number on them and blue pants were the fashion of choice. I tried to stay calm as I waited for Mom to enter, but my heart beat faster and faster, I still felt like I couldn't breathe. As much as I wanted to see her, I also was afraid. In my dream world, she ran out in her cute jeans and flowery blouse, hair freshly washed, makeup on, and said, "I'm coming home, baby, I'm coming home." The glass between us wouldn't exist, so she'd give me the huge hug I craved and we'd go get pancakes at some nearby diner to celebrate. She'd order a large stack with strawberries and whipped cream. I'd order the pancakes made with a happy face of fruit on top, just like we did every year on the last day of school to celebrate the freedom of summer. But this time, we'd celebrate freedom from jail.

Of course, my dream crashed before me when Mom entered in a dull blue uniform, her hair straggly, eyes weary.

"Be strong," Jared said. He squeezed my hand. "I'm going to wait in the car. I think you two should have time alone."

I was too stunned by everything to think about arguing. He gently let go of my hand and patted my shoulder. I faced her and felt like I couldn't budge, like the air between us was heavy and thick, pushing me back.

I walked to the stool in front of where she sat, put my hand on the glass to meet her hand on the other side. It was cold, hard, almost unbearable. I pushed back tears that wanted to flow from my eyes. I didn't want to cry. I needed to be strong.

"Hi, sweetheart," she said. "It's so good to see you. You look as beautiful as ever. Are you doing okay?" Her voice crackled, hoarse, like she'd been screaming a lot. Her lips looked chapped, her eyes redder than ever as I saw her up close.

"Yeah, Mom, I'm doing okay." I hated lying to the person I used to tell everything. But she hadn't been that person for a while, since she became too busy, too distracted, too stressed and then depressed, or to sum all that up, for the past two years, since Richard. "How are you?"

"Oh, I'm all right. It's not so bad," she said, pushing the straggles of brown hair from her eyes, the way she did when she wasn't telling the truth. "I don't have to worry about what outfit to wear, as you can see." There it was, her attempt to make things look positive when they were absolutely horrible.

"So, do you have any news on your case? Do you have a lawyer? Is anyone helping you so you can get out of here soon?" I asked. I knew I didn't have much time to visit; the security guard told us we had forty minutes. I didn't want to waste time.

Mom's green eyes gazed downward. She took a deep breath,

stared back at me for a moment, and turned away again. Why was she hesitating? What was she afraid to tell me?

"Mom, did you hear my question?"

"Yes, honey. I did, and no, I don't have anyone helping me other than the investigator and attorney assigned by the courts."

"Okay, well, that's two someones. Are they any good? Do they know you and have time for you? Are they doing anything? And what about Richard? Has he called you or is he still mysteriously and conveniently gone?"

"No, I haven't spoken with Richard."

"Of course you haven't, Mom. He's the reason you're here, isn't he? You're protecting him and you got caught. It's not right." I felt like the adult who needed to snap sense into the irresponsible child.

Mom looked around at the other inmates, then the guards, like she was afraid they could hear our conversation, but I didn't care. It wasn't like we were among a bunch of innocents, right?

"Richard is not the reason I'm here, Em. I am here for what I have done. I made my own choices, bad ones . . ."

My body prickled with heat. I felt the breath being choked from my lungs. She couldn't be admitting guilt. That wasn't possible.

"Mom, what are you saying? Are you kidding?"

"No, honey, I'm not kidding. I am so sorry, but Richard did not force me to take drugs." She paused and looked at me intently, as if there was something she needed me to understand. "He didn't force me to do any of the things I'm charged with."

What was she talking about? The drug-free queen willingly taking and dealing drugs? No way!

I shook my head violently. "No, I don't believe you. You're just lying to protect him because you think you have to, that you can't live without him. There's no way that's what you did." Sweat dripped down the back of my neck, my sweatshirt clinging tight and hot on my skin. I inhaled what smelled like a combination of some sort of cleaner, probably used on the blinding white floors, along with a musty smell that I guessed came from deep within the walls somewhere.

"Honey, I hate admitting this to you, but yes, I did." She had that desperate, sorry look on her face that made me want to punch the glass between us and shake sense into her.

"Mom, you were in charge of the drug-free campaign at my school! What are you saying to me?" Tears poured down my face. This was not how I pictured our visit. I wanted to come up with a way to prove her innocence, brainstorm some ideas to solve this mess. I thought she was wrongly accused and arrested, and here she was, telling me she was actually guilty. How could that be? I couldn't believe it, didn't want to believe it.

"Em, I know this is all so shocking and difficult to understand. I didn't mean to continue it, the OxyContin I mean. I tried it once to feel better. Remember how I would just be paralyzed with pain after a long shift at the hospital? The doctors thought it was fibromyalgia or something, but they had no cure. Well, that pill finally made me feel better, and it was easy for me to get them at work. I didn't mean to take them forever, didn't think I'd get hooked, but I did. I was stupid."

Her hands trembled, her face covered with beads of sweat. I wondered now if she was nervous or withdrawing from drugs.

"Why didn't you get help if you knew you were hooked? And why would you sell them when you know what they do to people, Mom? You always taught these things, and then you went and did them yourself?"

"I thought I was fine. I didn't realize how hooked I was. And when we needed money because Richard's business was in trouble, we started to sell. It was only supposed to be a one- or two-time thing, to get us out of debt, keep us from losing the house, but it got out of hand. We needed more money each month to keep up with unpaid bills. I didn't want to lose everything. I wanted to be able to give you things."

I listened and wondered how she could be okay with the excuses she spit out. Would that have worked for me if the roles were reversed? No way. Then I thought about the way we lived the past year. I remembered when Mom told me I didn't need to use the babysitting money I'd saved in a jar to buy new shoes, how she started to offer money so I could go out with friends when she had to leave at night to work. Now I knew what kind of work. I stared down at my white Vans, dirtier from six months of wear, but even dirtier now that I knew how they were bought.

"How did you sell them, Mom?" I tried to speak quieter now, not wanting anyone to hear any possible hint of guilt.

"I gave them to Richard. He and Jimmy sold them."

Jimmy's face flashed in my mind, the image of Richard's good buddy at our front door, his crooked smile with yellow teeth, his dirty blond hair, stringy strands that fell in his eyes as he talked way too fast. His hands always fidgeted—propped on his hips, scratching his head, rubbing his chin, then finally settling under his armpits with his arms crossed.

"Jimmy?" I said, horrified. "He's disgusting!"

She squirmed in her chair. Her hand shook when she lifted it to wipe a tear from her face. I hated this—her sadness, her weakness that made me feel sorry for her and angry all at the same time.

"So, you said Richard and Jimmy sold them. So, where are they? Why are they running around free while you're sitting here being punished? A good fiancé would have helped you stay away from drugs, found another way to earn money. But he's selfish. Maybe you can't do anything to find him while you're in jail, Mom, but I can. I can find him. I can prove that he forced you to help him and you can get out of here."

Mom put her hand on the window. If the window wasn't

there, she would have grabbed my hand, squeezed it tight between hers and hugged me close.

"Em, you need to stay out of this. It's very dangerous to get involved. Please promise me you'll let it go. If I cooperate and have good behavior, I'll get out sooner."

"Sooner? What's sooner? A few months? A year?"

Mom looked down, hesitated. "The attorney says ten years is common."

My stomach tied in painful knots. Images of boyfriends, prom, high school graduation, college, flashed before me. How would I do these things without her? "Mom, I'll be twenty-five. You'll miss my entire teenage life: my first date, probably my first break-up, all my high school dances, my track meets, listening to me talk about all my girl drama, applying to college, going to college, my first real job." When I stopped blurting out this movie reel of my life, all I saw was my mom, both hands up on the screen, tears rolling down her face.

"I'm so sorry," she stuttered through tears.

I placed my hands to hers on the glass. They were exactly like hers, no longer smaller, but exactly the same size and shape. How did two people who were so similar become so different?

# –11–

The visit with Mom ended abruptly with the announcement from a guard that visiting hours were over. I followed the trail of visitors out the door, a march of slouched sadness that passed from the jail walls to the blazing sun outside. I usually appreciated the sun's heat on my face on a cool February day. But today it stung, burned my cheeks, forced me to squint my eyes. It was too bright for a day like this. It should be cloudy, dreary, dark.

I peeked in the open window of the truck where Jared had been waiting for me. He was asleep, his head tilting back against the seat, his mouth opened wide in heavy breath. The aroma of peanut butter sandwiches in the bag Grandma packed also felt out of place in spite of my hunger. A picnic was too happy, too much like the mom I used to know.

"I hate her," I blurted when I opened the door.

Jared jolted awake and looked at me, wide eyed.

"No, you don't." He rubbed his eyes, closed them tight and opened them again, trying to wake up.

I climbed into the truck. "I do, Jared. I hate that woman in jail. She's not my mom. She's someone different, who makes my life miserable, someone selfish and careless and greedy."

"Em, I know you're mad. I'm mad too, at her and my dad.

But I can't let my dad's screw ups become my problems. I have to let them go, move on."

I slammed the door, stared straight ahead. "I don't think I can. I've always wanted to be her. I still do, but not the person I saw today." I slammed my fist against the door. "I want my real mom back, but that real mom wasn't who I thought she was." I finally got why Jared sometimes had his outbursts. There was no way to hold all this mess inside.

Jared placed his hand on my shoulder, like he always did to calm me down. "I wished for my dad to be a different person for years. I guess that's why I don't want to find him. I'm happier without him."

"Was your dad always messed up? Is it easy for you to say that because you never really liked him anyway?"

"Uh, no. When I was little, he'd play ball with me, tell jokes, take me to the beach, the park. He changed when my mom died. He stopped working, lost his job, started drinking, met Jimmy. I got used to him being gone. When he was home, he was always angry, mean. I try to keep the good dad in my head, but I'm not waiting for that guy anymore."

When we finally pulled up the gravel driveway at Grandma's house, the sun had begun to set, my legs felt restless, my jeans stuck to me, and my aching stomach reminded me I should have eaten those sandwiches. Grandma was outside, pulling weeds. She looked up and waved to us. She was the only person I ever saw who smiled while weeding. She stood frozen in her spot as we exited the truck and walked toward her.

"So, how'd it go? You kids okay?"

I didn't know why she asked that or how I was supposed to answer. Was I okay? Really?

"Well, I got to hear Mom tell me she's guilty and that she'll probably miss out on the entire rest of my childhood. I got to drive past our hometown and pretend it was normal to keep on driving. So, yeah, it was great, the time of my life."

Grandma looked like she'd been slapped. I couldn't stay and look at her, to see one more sad, disturbed person who couldn't do anything to change my situation. I trudged up the porch, into Grandma's house, feeling like the big bad wolf that ate grandma yet still felt hungry enough to pounce on Little Red Riding Hood or anyone else who crossed my path. I headed straight to the bedroom, plopped onto my bed, and cried like I hadn't cried in years. It was the kind of cry I couldn't control, sobs that came forcefully, made my chest hurt, my eyes sting, soaked the pillow, and left me heaving short, winded breaths. I lifted my head when I heard a familiar voice.

"Sometimes pie helps." I saw Ginny in my doorway, holding a pie, no longer in the sweaty, tight fitted running outfit. Instead, her hair was down, straight and sleek, falling just below her shoulders, and she wore a short, denim mini skirt, a Pine View High Basketball sweatshirt, and cowboy boots. Surprisingly, it all came together quite well on her.

I sat up, a little embarrassed for her to see me like that, a sad baby in a pool of tears. "Sorry, not such a good day for me."

"Yeah, I heard. Jared told me you visited your mom. No apology needed. I'd be locked in my room screaming if I were you."

"Well, thanks for the pie. Do you have some crazy, psychic ability that helps you know to bring pie to pathetic people like me?"

She laughed, "Uh, no, I don't, although that would be a cool power. I actually made it to welcome you to the neighborhood. New people don't come around often around here. Usually I have to find some other excuse to give baked goods away rather than eat them myself."

"Thanks, I don't think I've ever received a welcome pie." I stood up and took it from her. The smell of apples and cinnamon, plus the warmth of the dish in my hands reminded me of my hungry stomach. "I think I could eat the whole thing right now. I'm starving."

"Well, how about dinner and then pie? I was about to head over to Rusty's Pizza. My mom can take us."

"Sure, that sounds great. Or, Jared can take us if that's okay with your mom. He's probably as hungry as me."

"Even better. Then my mom can't tell me I only have an hour before she heads off to bed. She always tells me that, picks me up way too early, and then when I get home she stays up for two more hours. I don't get it."

"She's pulling a mom trick. She obviously doesn't want you to be out late, but if she admits that, she knows you'll get mad for not trusting you. So, she says she's going to bed so that if you want a ride, you'll either stay home or let her get you earlier."

"Hmm, I never thought of that. You're pretty smart, ya know?"

"Yeah well, clearly not smart enough to figure out my own mom. I thought I knew all her tricks, but apparently she had a few more than I realized."

Ginny had no response to that, just a sympathetic smile, and then said, "That's why there's pie. Nothing tricky about it at all, just plain old good stuff."

That was just what I needed to hear. A comment that didn't tell me all would be fine, chin up, stay strong, blah, blah, blah, but a simple statement about pie to tell me yes, my life kind of sucked, but at least I had a friend.

# –12–

It felt like years since I had gone out with friends. It made me remember why friends matter so much. You can have the worst possible day ever, but a good friend makes you forget about it, at least for a little while. They're like mini vacations from reality. I could tell Ginny was one of those friends. First of all, anyone who brought me a welcome pie had to be placed high on my list. But aside from that, she was so genuine and real, not afraid to be herself. I needed a friend like that.

"Nice truck you got, Jared. I especially like the roomy backseat, designed especially for bodies like mine," Ginny placed her hands on her hips, lifted her chin, flipped her hair, clearly poking fun at herself. While I knew she didn't love her body type, I loved that she didn't act all insecure about it. She almost flaunted it.

"I know, sorry, it's not much of a luxury ride back there. Em, do you want to sit in the back?"

Ginny lifted her eyes at me, smiled, winked, which clearly told me she wanted me to agree so she could be closer to Jared.

"Sure, I'll take backseat," I said. "Only because she made us dessert, though," I smiled and climbed in.

We pulled into a crowded parking lot at Rusty's Pizza Parlor. It was one of five restaurants in town, the others being

McDonald's, Express Chinese Restaurant, Larry's Sandwich Shop, and Old Town Coffee Shop. This was a drastic switch from the many choices of restaurants back home. Apparently, Rusty's was the happening spot. We drove past three kids who looked our age on Ginny's side of the car. They leaned against an old asphalt-colored mustang. The scrawny one of the three blew a puff of cigarette smoke out and stared into our window, said something as he nudged the tall redhead with arms about the size of my waist. The guy with brown, stringy hair and a chain dangling at the middle of his tank-topped chest glared at us. On Jared's side, a huddle of about ten moved toward the middle of the aisle so Jared had to slow down. He inched forward slowly, stepping on and off the brake. I heard a loud bang on the back of Jared's truck and someone yell, "Hey! Move a little quicker! Your hunk of metal junk is in our way!"

"What the heck?" Jared said, slamming on his breaks.

"Hey, don't worry about it. They're just being idiots. If you make a big deal of it, things will only get worse. Trust me. Play it cool," Ginny said.

Jared pulled forward slowly. "I really want to go bust that guy's hand. If it happens again, I'm not gonna be quiet."

Ginny looked at me with a relieved glance. I got the feeling she was a little afraid of these people, in spite of her air of calm. Jared found a parking spot two rows away from the crowd. As soon as we climbed out of the truck, I felt nervous, that feeling of being the new kid, where everyone stared. I didn't like it, and I wasn't really used to it. I was the one back home who knew people, not the most popular girl in school, but I had a decent number of friends. Plus, I didn't stand out at home, blended right in with everyone else. I wasn't the one who people poked fun at. Here, I had a feeling it would be different. As we approached another group, I wanted to crawl under one of the cars and hide, or magically warp to the inside of the restaurant. I heard the giggles of three girls as they pushed their heads closer together, whispered and peered over at us. They reminded me of the mean girls at my school back home, wearing enough dark eyeliner and lip gloss to keep the make-up industry strong for decades, and showing enough skin and curves to keep every boy turning their heads for a free show. Some of them looked pretty, but they were really vultures that honed in on their prey, attacking anything nearby with biting words, piercing stares, and shrieking laughter. As we passed, I saw a plastic cup hit Ginny in the back. Dark liquid and ice splattered and hit the ground. Ginny's back arched, and she spun around to the crowd of people in a huddle, the three girls obviously hidden in the middle.

"Seriously? Are you kidding me? Which one of you stupid wimps thinks you're so cool to throw a drink at someone?" Ginny yelled, clearly not afraid of them at this moment.

"You talkin' to us, Giant Ginny?" It was the skinny boy with the cigarette. I knew he was a jerk. Jared stepped forward.

"Should she be talking to you, idiot? Are you the two-year-old who can't hang on to his sippy cup?" Jared picked the cup up from the ground, swung it at him, "Here you go." The cup blazed like a fast ball across the space between us and them, whacked Cigarette Jerk in the forehead, before landing back on the pavement.

"Oh, you've messed up big time, Jailbird Boy." Cigarette Jerk pulled away from the crowd, stood square in front of Jared. He was significantly smaller than Jared, but had no fear. He was as stupid as he looked. He shoved Jared in the chest.

"What did you call me?" Jared asked and pushed him back.

"Jailbird Boy, that's your new name. You used to live in the same house as a convicted criminal, right? And that right there? That girly girl? We've dubbed her Jail Baby, as we figure like mother like daughter, she'll be next."

I stood in that parking lot in a head spin of rage and tears. How did they all know about my mom? I wanted to jump on that stupid, smoky boy and rip his tongue out so he couldn't use it to cut people's hearts anymore. What was wrong with people like him? In two minutes he had humiliated three people. And it wasn't like he looked so cool himself, his greasy hair, his bloodshot eyes, skinny arms that Jared could snap in two. A weasel. That's what he was, that gawky, annoying animal I learned about in third trade. I don't know what made me do it, but I felt saliva build in my mouth, I let it build up, and then I spat at him. It hit his short, stubby leg.

Jared and Ginny turned and looked at me, shock on their faces. If I could have stared at myself that way I would have. I had never spit at someone. I definitely wasn't the model of a classy girl right then and there, but I didn't care. If you were spit on, you were worth nothing. That's what I wanted him to feel, like nothing.

"Eww, gross!" I heard one of the blonde girls say. "Get a grip or go back to the scummy place you came from."

Apparently they didn't feel like nothing. I realized I probably looked like some lowly scum, but whatever.

"You guys don't know anything about us. You think you do. You think you know who I am and can sit here and judge. But you have no idea what my story is, or where I'm from, or what I'm capable of. And if you were dropped smack into my hometown with no one you knew, you'd never make it. Come on, Ginny, Jared. I think we can find somewhere more "classy" to eat than this piece of crap."

I wanted to walk away, but unfortunately, we had to pass by them again on the way to our truck.

Cigarette Jerk gave us a glare that said he was going to do something. Jared moved to the right side of Ginny and me, to block the evil eyes from us. He was big enough to do that. I couldn't see his face, but I knew what he was doing. He was puffed up, piercing them back with his own scary look, daring them to try something. Lucky for us, a cop car drove by, so if they were about to start a fight, they changed their minds. But as soon as we passed, I heard spitting. First one, then another, then more. I felt one hit the back of my head. My heart raced, I wanted to scream, but I bit my lip, kept my head high. They were trying to make me feel like nothing, but they didn't know me. This made me want to prove I was something.

# -13-

We ended up at the yellow arches for dinner, the drive-thru because none of us wanted to get out of the car and be noticed. I ordered a Filet-O-Fish sandwich. Jared and Ginny gave me the same look they gave me when I spit.

"I know it sounds weird, but I used to get them all the time when I was a kid, probably five, during that happy time of my life when I thought the world was perfect with a Filet-O-Fish and an orange drink."

"You want an orange drink too?" Jared asked, his nose scrunched in that "eww" sort of way.

"No, I'll just have a coke." I had to do something they thought was normal, or something that even I thought was normal. I was starting to feel a little bit crazy. It scared me.

"Hey, can you order a Big Mac for my friend as long as you don't mind dropping by his house? It's on the way back to your place. And I'd like a Quarter Pounder combo meal."

Jared placed our orders and we rolled through the drive-thru like it was any ordinary teenage day. In reality, it was a far cry from that for me. I normally looked forward to biting into the greasy, soul satisfying fare of fast food. But this time, I worried nothing would actually bring comfort.

While we waited, I figured it was a good time to ask Ginny

the question I'd been wondering about since we left Rusty's.

"So, Ginny, how did everyone know about my mom in jail? How did they know who we were?"

She looked surprised by my question. "Your grandma must not have shown you the article in the local paper that's delivered to everyone for free."

"Uh, no, she hasn't. I had no idea she even got a paper."

She took a breath, let it out. "Okay, well, your story was in there. My parents showed it to me the day after I met you."

I felt angry, humiliated. How was that okay for reporters to spread my personal life all over without asking me about it?

"Wow, that's embarrassing. And wrong. No one even talked to us. What did the article say?"

"It wasn't that bad. It mostly talked about your mom, not you guys, said she used to live here, ran track in high school, was in student government, basically all good stuff about her. It mentioned the drug charges and said her daughter and fiancé's son would be living here with the grandmother. That's pretty much it."

"Well, the story obviously made us look like horrible people by the way everyone treated us tonight. And how did they even know it was us? Were our pictures in the news?"

Ginny nodded. "Pretty cute ones actually, but I know that probably doesn't matter to you."

I felt like someone must feel when their house has been robbed, completely violated. I thought coming to the middle of nowhere would at least give us the chance to be invisible, but clearly not.

"Hey, don't let those idiots get to you. I saw the news story and it didn't make me want to avoid you. They're always looking for someone to pick on. You're new, so you're an easy target. You could have been the prom queen or daughter of the president and they'd still find a reason to bring you down."

I could only nod back to her. I didn't have words I could

speak without tears coming with them. I swallowed hard to hold them back and keep it together.

After we got our food, Jared asked, "So, we're stopping at your friend's?"

"Oh, yeah, I'd love for him to meet you guys. He's my good friend and prom date, Chris. He's super cool."

I wanted to ask why on earth she would like to introduce us to anyone cool when we were obviously the town's dirt, but Jared spoke first.

"Sure, just tell me where to go." I was surprised he didn't say anything about the news story, but his expression kind of gave me the answer. He looked tired and defeated, a look I didn't see on him often.

"Turn here," Ginny said. "It's the third house on the left." The only good thing I'd noticed about this speck of a town was how easy it was to get around. Everything flowed off one main street so far, and it seemed there weren't even that many streets to travel. Ginny hopped out of the truck when Jared pulled up to the curb. "I'll be right back," she said.

A couple minutes later, Ginny skipped down the lawn, her arm entwined with a tall tanned boy who laughed loudly as Ginny enthusiastically talked and gazed up at him. I was impressed with how quickly Ginny had let go of any anger from the pizza place.

The chilly night air blew in as Ginny opened the truck door. "Jared, Emily? Meet Chris, master of Big Mac eating, Guitar Hero, and slayer of those lovelies we met tonight. If he would have been with us, they would have at least been burned by Chris's ruthless comebacks.

"Hey," he said, flipping his ash blond hair off his forehead. The glow from the streetlight revealed the most incredible blue eyes. "Nice to meet you guys. Ginny told me what happened at Rusty's. Sorry our town is so frickin' stupid. I'm embarrassed to admit I was born in the same place as those losers you saw tonight."

He reached his hand out to me. I grabbed it, as he firmly grasped back. He wasn't Jared handsome, but his smile pretty much made me melt into my seat. It was also nice to see someone else who didn't like the crowd we just encountered.

"Thanks for the food. I'm starving. My dad made some weird casserole thing. I pretended I liked it and fed it to the dog. If she dies tonight, I wouldn't be surprised."

*Finally, a good reason to laugh*, I thought. I wondered if his dad always made his dinner, or if his mom wasn't around. I didn't want to ask that after just meeting him. Maybe I was secretly hoping there were other cool people with messed up families like mine. Then I wouldn't feel so weird.

"So, where are we going?"

"I don't know, good question," Ginny said. "We don't really want to go where there's a chance of running into anyone. My mom and dad are on their usual Friday "date night," so we can't go to my house. They don't like anyone over when they aren't home, as Chris knows."

"We can probably go to my grandma's. I don't think she'd mind, although I can't say I know her well enough to really know that." I don't know what made me say that. I'd apparently lost my mind.

"That's okay with me, plus we've got pie there," Ginny said.

I thought I might really need that apple pie if Grandma was her normal self. I could just grab the pie and head to bed, hide under the sheets with my journal and a flashlight and eat the whole thing, but that would have gained me status as socially awkward, not exactly what I was trying to achieve with Ginny and Chris.

When we pulled in the driveway, we heard music blasting from inside the house. I didn't figure Grandma as the party type, but decided anything was possible based on what we'd seen of her so far. When we got out of the truck though, I could tell it wasn't a party. The music was much too mellow, a soft, crooning voice bellowing out. Before I opened the door, I saw candles lit in the windows, on the dining table, all other lights dimmed or out. I opened the door, and the words blasted loud and clear, with Grandma's voice swooning over it in a pitch better suited to a sick coyote.

"I love you, Lord. You are my savior. I looooooove you, Lord," Grandma sang with her arms lifted, her eyes shut. I looked at Chris, then Ginny, as smiles crept upon their faces, and then Jared, who shook his head and lifted one eye at me as if to say, "Wow, totally crazy."

Somehow I managed to talk, in spite of my shock and embarrassment. "Hey, we're back!"

Grandma opened her eyes, jumped a little. "Oh, I'm sorry. I didn't hear you come in. I get so engrossed in my music and the Lord, can't help myself. He just takes me away." She scurried over to her 1980's stereo system and pushed a little silver lever down to stop the cassette player. I'd heard about those, but never saw one in real life. "So, what can I get you kids? Anything? How was pizza? What you have in those bags looks more like burgers."

"Yeah, we sort of changed our mind about pizza," I glanced at Ginny and Chris, hoping they wouldn't share what really went down.

"More like the entire teenage population of this pit town changed our minds about pizza," Ginny said.

Grandma's eyes widened, the way they did before she was about to layer on the advice or tell a story. "Really? Well how did they do that? If you all want pizza, you should have pizza. What happened?"

We each stared at each other, like we wanted the other person to talk. I didn't really want to tell Grandma what happened. I didn't know her well enough to know how she'd react. If I told Mom what'd happened, she probably would have driven down to the pizza restaurant and told off any or every teen she saw, guilty or not. I didn't need any more negative attention drawn to me.

"It was nothing, really," I said, "just normal obnoxious teen stuff and too crowded. The drive-thru was easier."

Grandma looked unconvinced. Here we go, I thought. She's going to ask a bunch of questions, like every parent, to get the truth out.

Instead, she just kept the same look and said, "Okay, well, as long as you got what you want, I guess all is well. There's always a reason for everything. God must have wanted you to have a burger tonight."

I was surprised she could connect burgers to God. I didn't mention to her the fact that I was eating fish. I remembered that story from Sunday School, when I was in Kindergarten. The teacher had this flannel board in front of her with blue fabric for the ocean and tan for the sand. She told the story of Jesus feeding five thousand people from only a few loaves of bread and a handful of fish. I thought that was amazing. How did he do that?

"Well, make yourselves at home. I have plenty to do, won't be in your way."

"Thanks," Jared said. "We'll try to stay out of your way too." He walked to the kitchen table and set his McDonald's bag down. We followed him there, like little lambs following their shepherd. Shoot, now I was making Biblical references.

Although Grandma tried to stay out of our way, her presence was very apparent.

She sat on the couch, only about twenty feet from the kitchen, which was divided only by a partial wall. We sat and inhaled our food, all of us apparently too hungry to carry on a conversation. Between the gulps of soda and chomping of fries, hamburgers, and one fish sandwich, we clearly heard, "Blessed are the poor in spirit, for theirs is the kingdom of heaven. Blessed are those who mourn, for they will be comforted.

Blessed are the meek, for they will inherit the earth."

She continued on with the senseless description of who are the blessed. It seemed so false, so far from the truth. Those who are poor in spirit and meek are the blessed ones? I wanted no part of that blessing.

"So, you guys starting school here?" Chris asked. I did say a *Thank God* in my head right then and there for someone choosing to talk over Grandma. Silence always felt awkward around people I didn't know very well, but silence plus crazy talk from Grandma equaled sheer humiliation.

"Uh, I don't really know. Maybe?" I looked at Jared to see if he had a better answer. His mouth was stuffed with food. He looked at me, raised his eyebrows and shrugged his shoulders to let me know he didn't know either.

"I guess we need to figure that out. This might sound weird, but I actually don't like missing school. Although, starting at a new school doesn't sound like a fun plan. I really just wanna go home and go back to my old life, no offense to you guys."

"Hey, no offense taken." Ginny said. "I'd hate to start over in a new place, not that my current situation is so hot. My social existence consists of Chris. He has a few more friends, but neither of us have been homecoming king or queen candidates, or the ones who everyone wants to sit near at lunch, or the ones who get gawked at by the opposite sex for our cover model good looks."

I actually thought Chris could be, and Ginny wasn't a cover model, but she was pretty with her near perfect skin, caramel tan, and super thick eyelashes even without any mascara. But of course, most people in this town saw her size and chose to ignore the rest of her. I hated that.

"Well, I'd hang out with you guys, either here or back at my home. You guys are pretty chill." I nodded to Ginny.

Ginny smiled and nudged Chris, "Aww, did you hear that, Chris? We finally have some friends. Well, if you do start school here, hopefully we can get at least one class together. Our school isn't that big, so we probably will."

"I hope so, but if not, I hope I get a class with Cigarette Jerk. We clearly have a very strong connection."

That got a laugh from everyone. Ah, laughter with friends, I hoped that kept coming.

# -14-

My conflict about whether to register at Pine View High ended after Ginny and Chris left. I relaxed into Grandma's recliner in the dimly lit living room, pulled a white knit throw blanket over my legs and stared at my phone that had apparently shut off at some point that evening. I wanted to cry. Even with a belly full of junk food, I still had a wrenching, empty feeling. The only connection to my world back home was now dead, useless, unable to help me escape from my current reality. So, when Grandma told Jared and me that she called the school while we were visiting Mom, and we were all set to start Monday morning, I gripped my phone tight, pushed the power button over and over with my thumb even though I knew that wouldn't do anything other than keep me from throwing it across the room and shattering the screen to pieces.

"I don't want you to get behind in your studies, kids, and since we don't know how long you'll be with me, I figured I should get you back in the classroom as soon as possible. It might help to take your mind off things, meet some friends." Grandma eyed us closely, her fingers intertwined together in a tight grip that showed she was nervous.

Jared stood up from the couch abruptly, put his hands on his hips and said, "Hey, I don't mean to be rude, but isn't there any way we could stay on at school back home? I know you were told to take care of us, but we could probably stay with friends back home, at least to finish out the school year. It seems so crazy that we need to start over here." He looked like he did before a basketball game, all serious, ready to take on whatever came at him.

Grandma peered up at him, took a deep breath, let it out. "Jared, I know this is all so upsetting. Really, I do. But I can't go back on what Tiffany asked me to do. She's my daughter, and we've had too many falling outs as it is. I need to help her. I need to let her count on me and not mess up. And what kind of grandma would I be if I told Emily to go back home and find someone else to take her in? I know you're not family, Jared, but you're a young man who needs a mom or a grandma as much as anyone else. I really am trying my best to help you two."

Jared stood frozen with his hands still on his hips, but his expression softened, kind of like a wounded puppy. He shook his head, then looked at me. I knew he was trying to get us out of this, but I also knew he understood what Grandma was saying. In spite of how much I didn't want to start school at Pine View either, I knew she was right. It really was hard to be mad at her.

"I get that you need to help Mom, and I don't want to fall behind with school. But I hope we can easily go back to our old school as soon as Mom is out of jail." I hated the thought of a new school, but I didn't see that we had much of a choice, about anything actually.

"Of course you can, dear. I know this isn't what you want, any of it." She looked at me with her sparkling green eyes that seemed to be holding back tears.

Jared sat back down with a sigh of defeat. "Okay, well, new school it is then." He glanced at me with a look that said, "Hey, I tried," which I knew was also because he didn't want to start over either. But like he always did, he rolled with the punches that came his way.

Ginny asked me to go to the mall with her Saturday to help her pick out a dress for prom, which turned out to be a really good distraction from my real life problems. We laughed a lot while trying on both the cute and ridiculous outfits we found, and then couldn't stop laughing over pretty much everything after eating way too much sugar at the candy store where we tried way too many free samples. But once I returned to Grandma's later that afternoon, the rest of the weekend went painfully slow. I thought about calling Ginny again, to talk or maybe plan something else, but realized I couldn't even get her number since it was held hostage in my dead phone. I thought about going for a run, but I didn't want to be seen by anyone. I thought about driving over to Chris's house, since we knew where he lived, but Jared and I both thought that might make us look a little desperate for friendship. So, I spent the rest of the weekend trying not to stress about starting Pine View High School.

The highlight of Sunday was probably when Jared and I sat on the front porch before dinner. The setting sun created a brilliant orange glow in the sky, the trees surrounding Grandma's dirt lot rustled in the breeze and blew a scent of pine our way. Jared strummed a tune on his guitar, and I vented in my journal. I wrote about how the sky at Grandma's was beautiful, like the sky back home that hovered over my neighborhood every night, streamed light into my bedroom window while I finished my homework, turned dark as Jared and I played a video game or talked about our friends on our big comfy living room couch. This sky did that too. It hung over us and dazzled us with its beauty, reminding me that some things could remain good, like the sky, and music from a guitar, and Jared.

After dinner, Grandma told us we were to meet with our

counselor at 7:45 in the morning to get our schedules, so we headed to bed without a lot of hope for a good night's sleep. I spent an hour lying in bed thinking of all the things that could go wrong, knowing I'd probably be greeted with a crowd like the one I had at the pizza place. If my phone had been working, I would have texted Ginny, told her to meet me somewhere. I hoped I'd get a class with her or Chris, and I hoped I wouldn't embarrass them.

I awoke the next morning from a dream that left me dreading my day even more. In my dream, I walked down the red-bricked school's barren hallway, a pit in my stomach. The final bell had already rung, so I knew all eyes would be on me when I entered my first classroom. My steps were loud on the cement pavement, teacher talk drifted from the doors I passed, "So, after mixing the chemicals, note the reaction in your lab book, then . . ."

I was almost there, English class, luckily a class I understood. I placed my hand on the cold metal door handle, turned it, pushed the door open as it made a loud creek. So much for trying to enter quietly. I took a deep breath, but instead of forty pairs of eyes on me, I saw three—my mom, a boy I didn't recognize, and Chris, who oddly was the teacher. My mom sat at the front, head down, pen scribbling wildly across the pages of a journal. Chris stood at a podium, leafed through a high school literature book that was the size of a small child. "Aha, yes, that's what we want," he said, "a bit of Shakespeare to start us off." He looked up and froze his eyes on mine. "Oh, it looks like we have a new student. You must be Emily Greene." His smile was a wide welcome sign.

"Yes, I am." In my dream I wanted to laugh and say, "Chris? Why are you up there teaching?" But of course in dreams, as weird as they get, you just go with them, like it's all normal. Plus, he had a British accent, which always charmed me and made me think the person speaking it was authentic and important.

His was one that seemed forced and fake, but he stayed consistent with it, so again, as in all dreams, I went with it.

My mom looked up after Chris spoke. I wanted to say, "Hey, Mom!" I felt so happy to see her, waited for her to jump up, give me that warm, familiar smile, watch her eyes light up like they always did when she hadn't seen me in a while, then embrace me with a hug. She didn't do that. She looked up from her journal, gave me half a smile, moved a backpack out of the aisle so I could get by her, and dove back into her journal. My heart sank. I stood frozen.

"So, why don't you take a seat, Emily?" Chris swept his hands out at the empty desks, encouraging me to pick one.

The walls narrowed in on me, closer and closer, about to squeeze me in if they went any further, where I'd be stuck, choked, unable to shout to my mom for help. The other boy, who sat still all this time looked like someone I had seen in old photographs. I looked closer, stared way more than a polite or even normal person should. He looked at me for a moment and stared me straight in the eyes. Then he smiled, nodded his head, and I knew who it was, my dad. He was the same dad in all those photos with my mom. I couldn't talk or move, the walls rushed in closer, and I woke up.

The dream only made me feel worse about school. Before I fell to sleep the night before, I tried to think of something positive about starting Pine View. What I came up with was the idea that maybe I would feel closer to my mom by attending her alma matter, that although I couldn't be with her physically, maybe I could be with her in spirit as I walked the same halls, entered the same doors, stared at the same walls she did when she was my age.

But when I opened my eyes from that dream, I had the emptiest feeling. Mom didn't know me. She didn't smile and run to hug me. She stared at me, vacant eyes, ho-hum expression. I was nothing to her. Nothing. The way I would soon be as she rotted in a jail cell, and I rotted in classrooms that made me think of how much I missed her and how much time ticked away while I did nothing to get her out. Instead of making kids with parents in jail go to school, we should be provided with classes on how to break your parents out of jail. School felt like a waste of time and a torture chamber.

My alarm blasted, which was completely unnecessary since I sat there awake already. I stared at the numbers, bright red, 6:45, not far from the time Mom was removed from me only a handful of days ago. I remembered her last hug, wrapped the blankets tight around me, tried to imagine her there holding me, telling me things would be okay. The bedroom door opened to push away that dream.

"Time to rise and shine," Grandma announced, way too happy. "I'm making breakfast, so come have a bite when you're ready. Jared, would you like some of that tea?" She yelled into his room.

I laughed under the blanket at that.

"No, not today, but thanks." I heard him grumble.

"Okay, I'll just have juice today for you then." She left, humming a tune, something about God again.

I grabbed my jeans and a white T-shirt, and headed toward the bathroom. I stopped at Jared's room first. "This ought to be good to wear, right? No color, no style, just me in my boring outfit that won't bring on any attention."

"Em, you could bring on attention in just about any outfit. Take a look in the mirror once in a while. You're not exactly plain Jane."

The compliment shocked me. Jared didn't comment on my looks much. And I didn't think of myself as anything out of the ordinary. Mom always called me beautiful, especially on days like this when I felt awkward and insecure. Maybe he was trying to take her place at that moment.

"Well, I don't agree with that, but thanks, Jared. I kind of needed to hear that right now, even though I still don't want any attention at all today."

It took me longer than I meant to get ready, not because I did much, but because I kept trying to figure out how people might see me. I stood in front of that mirror, as ordered by Jared, and tried to look at myself as a stranger would. I stared at my skin, spattered with light freckles on my nose, a couple small breakouts on my forehead that I covered with some make-up, wishing now I had bangs to cover them since the make-up didn't do a lot. I still didn't see beyond the ordinary in myself. Jared was obviously being nice.

By the time I got out of the bathroom, Jared was already dressed and on the last remaining bits of his breakfast. The table was set with oatmeal, a bowl of brown sugar to sweeten it, fresh berries, scrambled eggs, juice. I sat at the table and thought of Mom.

"Did you always make these nice breakfasts? Like when Mom was in school?" I asked since I never heard many positive words from Mom about her childhood.

"Well, not always. I started doing it when your mom was in high school. Before that I had some difficulty getting up early enough to make breakfast. Your mom was sort of on her own."

I didn't want to be too nosey, but I couldn't resist asking why. "Were you sick?"

"I guess you could say that. I was depressed. We had moved a lot because of your grandpa being in the military, so I never felt settled. I'd get attached to people and then had to say goodbye. Then I'd worry about your mom making new friends. I worried all the time; it wore me out. I slept a lot, never felt like doing anything. One day when your mom was about nine, a friend of mine dropped off your mom from school because she had started walking the five mile route home after waiting an hour for me to pick her up. I felt horrible, sobbed as she handed me a paper with the name and phone number of her church and told me I needed to get help. That was a wake-up call for me. So, I went to church, talked with a pastor, made appointments with a psychologist, got some medicine. It took a lot of time, years actually, but I got better.

One of the perks of your grandfather being in the military was he could retire after only twenty years and still receive pay. Your mom was about to start high school when he retired, so we thought this little town would be a safe and affordable place to settle. That was true, but I've never felt completely accepted here. I know people think I'm a little different, too religious or something, but I'm not going to change. My faith saved my life. I only wish I would have changed sooner, before I missed quality time with my young daughter."

I plopped a second spoonful of brown sugar onto my oatmeal, watched it melt, swirled it with my spoon, added some strawberries, bananas, nuts, another spoonful of sugar, and then another after that. It looked amazing, but after one bite I couldn't eat anymore. It was way too sweet and I wasn't hungry at all. I felt like I might throw up.

Grandma had described part of my life. I remembered when Mom started to forget me. It was around the time I started eighth grade. A friend's mom would see me walking after school and offer to take me home. I'd usually said no, told them I walked because I wanted to. I didn't want them to know my mom was asleep in her bed, or on the couch. When she snapped out of her mood, she always felt guilty. Then she acted way too nice, gave me more attention and things than I wanted or needed, like too much brown sugar in my oatmeal.

This all happened not long after Mom began dating Richard. She was so moody. I could never predict if she would be stressed, or relaxed, or happy, or miserable. Now I wondered if it was because she was on drugs, and I also worried she would never get better. Grandma was able to start over, but she wasn't in jail.

"Emily? Are you okay? Can I get you something different?

You don't seem to like your oatmeal much."

"Oh, no, sorry. I'm not very hungry. And, I think I put too much sugar on."

"Okay, well, here. At least try to eat this banana on the way or something. Your day will go better if you have something in your stomach." She handed me the banana and then held my hand. "And I'm praying for you, Em, and you too, Jared." She reached over and grabbed his hand. "I know today is going to be difficult, but God is on your side."

I didn't believe that he was on my side, but I thanked her anyway. Jared thanked her too, then we headed to his truck.

As we pulled into the school parking lot, I noticed the rows of flat-roofed buildings that looked a lot like Chaparral High back home, only trimmed with green paint instead of blue. Also similar was the sprawling chain-link fence that surrounded the school. We found a parking spot at the back of the lot that faced the track, but instead of the familiar bright green football turf, I noticed a patchy brown field. Empty chip bags and scraps of paper blew against the side of the fence, competing for an escape route along with the weeds that poked through the chain-link gaps. Before I got out of the truck, I scanned the people walking by in the rear-view mirror, hoping to see Ginny or Chris. I also looked for Cigarette Jerk and his groupies, although not because I wanted to see them. I wanted to avoid them. People fiddled with their hair, jostled their backpacks over their shoulders, chatted and laughed, or stared blankly and wearily toward the school gates, looking much like people back home, but I couldn't shout hello or name any of them.

We managed to walk through the parking lot unnoticed by anyone and found the front office. Once inside, we approached the counter with the attendance sign hanging above it. We stood and waited for a broad shouldered woman in a bright red top to notice us. She tapped the keys of her computer, wiggled and clicked the mouse a few times, grabbed a pencil and jotted something on a sticky note. She finally lifted her face and adjusted her glasses on her nose, looked up at us briefly, and then turned behind her to a younger lady with blonde, wavy hair who swirled a coffee stirrer in a Styrofoam cup and took a sip, also not acknowledging us.

"Did you see the e-mail from Mr. Smith?"

"No, I didn't. I can look now though."

"Yeah, I think you might want to check it."

I thought the bright-red-top-lady might actually speak to us, but no, she went back to her computer, clicked the mouse a few more times, then finally said, "Can I help you?" in an annoyed tone. If she was the person chosen to sit at the front of the office and greet people, I was worried. She could at least smile and try to be nice.

"Yeah, we need to get our class list. Today is our first day," I said, thinking maybe now she would decide to be nice since this small town probably didn't get many new students.

"You need to go right behind you to Mrs. Beam. She can help you." She looked down at her computer again, grabbed her best friend, the computer mouse, and still didn't smile. So much for warm welcomes.

Jared and I walked down a small, dark hallway, and I prepped myself for another grumpy encounter. To our right was a door with the name "Cassandra Beam" written on it, and as soon as I peeked in, I was surprised. A woman with long bleached blonde hair pulled into a high ponytail sat behind her small tidy desk. The walls were painted a bright yellow and covered with colorful artwork that appeared to have been created by her children or maybe students. Behind her rested a large bookshelf filled with thick novels and little knick-knacks like blue birds and owls. I noticed a stuffed bear holding a handmade sign that read "#1 Counselor" and a small framed print that proclaimed, "Make today your best day ever!" She talked into her phone in Spanish, very animated and enthusiastic, but unlike the other office lady, she managed to look up, smile, and motion us into her office.

We moved slowly to the two plastic chairs in front of her desk.

"Okay, gracias, gotta go." She clanked her phone down on her desk. "So sorry about that, how can I help you two?"

"Uhh, we're here to pick up our class lists. It's our first day today," Jared said.

"Oh yes, I spoke with your grandmother. Sweet lady!"

That was the first nice thing I had heard about my grandmother ever, unless I counted Ginny saying, "Hey, don't worry about it. We're all a little crazy," after I apologized for Grandma's loud singing and reading of Bible verses on the night we had McDonald's.

"So, last name is Greene, right?" Mrs. Beam said. She clicked onto her computer. "Okay, Emily, I'm printing your schedule first. And what is your last name, hon?" She asked Jared. "I didn't jot that down, just remember it was different from Emily's."

"It's Holder, Jared."

She clicked on her computer again and then said, "Okay, two schedules coming up. I hope you two have a great day and if you need anything, you come see me, all right?" She looked at us with big blue eyes, waiting for our response.

"Yes, we will. Thank you, Mrs. Beam." I smiled.

"Of course, no problemo, that's what I'm here for." She pulled two pieces of paper from the printer and handed them to us. "Emily, you start off in Mr. Brandt's English class, Building C, room 24. All the buildings are in alphabetical order with the letters printed on the wall. So, everything should be easy to find. Jared, you start in Room E5, Chemistry, Mrs. Krueger. Your lockers probably aren't the best, so if they need repair, let someone in the office know so they can call maintenance about it. And you'll be late for your first class, but don't worry. Your teachers will know you've just started. Okay guys, good luck, I hope you have your best day!"

I had never encountered such an enthusiastic counselor. I wondered if she also coached the cheerleading squad or something. At least she was better to talk to than angry-attendance-lady, who still stared at her computer as we passed, ignoring three students in line at the counter to talk to her.

Outside, it was quiet. I tried to enjoy the moment. This was the side of school I liked—the clean cut grass and manicured bushes, the sound of teachers' voices from open windows and doors, spilling knowledge and inspiration into the students who chose to take it. Weird, I know. Maybe this was *my* crazy, but I liked that. I liked learning and listening to people who knew more than me. But unfortunately, high school could be ruined with only a few disrespectful idiots, those who could care less about anyone but themselves, who laughed at failed papers and tests and anyone who didn't meet their "cool" status. That was what I worried about now, as we walked past the A building, then the B building, and then the dreaded C building, where I felt like my life was about to end in an onslaught of stares that felt like thousands of knives piercing my very insecure self as I entered the classroom.

"I really don't want to go in there," I said to Jared. I felt tears well up in my eyes, my throat choked up. *Don't cry*, I said to myself. Jared could read me. He knew I was about to lose it.

"Hey, Em," he pulled me toward him and hugged me. "It's gonna be okay. You're way better than any of these people, and if they don't give you a chance to show them how cool you are, it's their loss."

I wished I had his confidence. I wished I didn't care what anyone else thought of me. I wanted to stay in his protective hug, like I did when Mom was taken that horrible morning. But of course, I had to break out of it and try to call up glimpses of the hug in my mind throughout the day to make it through.

"Okay, I'll try to remember I'm cool, even if they all hate me."

"See you at lunch?"

"Definitely, by the office? That big tree?"

"Sure," he said. He smiled that brilliant smile of his, but even he looked a little nervous. I wasn't sure if that made me feel better, but at least it told me he was almost as human as me.

As I approached the classroom door, I remembered my dream, my mom's face, how she didn't know me. Maybe this was a classroom she sat in, I thought to myself. Maybe I would feel like she was with me today. I touched the handle, turned it slow, hoped no one would hear it. But of course, it creaked, and every face turned around and looked right at me, and fitting of my current charmed life, none of those faces were Ginny or Chris.

The teacher looked up from his book, "Welcome, my lady, to a day of Shakespeare. Please, take a seat right there in that only empty desk, next to Sir Anthony."

Seriously? They're studying Shakespeare? Like in my dream? I tried to smile at Sir Anthony, who looked up at me with one eye, his other covered with shaggy hair, but all I could think about was all the eyes on me as I walked what seemed like a slow marathon to my desk.

"All right, so I'll cut the Shakespeare for a moment. That should make you all happy to have a new student and give her a good ol' Pine View High welcome."

He set his book down, picked up a paper from his desk, "Let's see, ah, yes, Emily, Emily Greene, a fine name. We're happy to have you."

I hoped he wouldn't ask me to talk, to tell something about myself like teachers often did.

"So, let's all introduce ourselves, shall we? I'll start, and then we'll go around the room. If you have anything to add about yourself when everyone is done, Emily, then you can."

I looked at the clock, the number of students, and said

thanks to God for the first time in a while for the fact that there probably wouldn't even be enough time to get through the twenty or so sitting in this stifling room, let alone, leave time for me to talk.

I continued to feel relieved when I saw that Mr. Brandt was quite a talker. He spent at least five minutes talking about himself, then took about five more minutes to answer questions from students who were obviously trying to distract him so they wouldn't have to talk either. When the first student, with messy dark hair and a colorful tattoo covering his right forearm, introduced himself, there was only three minutes left in class, and Mr. Brandt still had to announce the homework, so Hector Gomez was the only name I learned. I was so glad I didn't have to talk. The bell rang when Mr. Brandt was mid-sentence into the homework. A few people stayed and listened, most stood up and walked out the door. I stayed in my seat, felt a bit frozen, like my legs couldn't take me to one more class.

Hector walked by me, smiled, handed me a note, "Welcome to PV."

"Thanks," I smiled, surprised that people were that nice here. But I opened the note to read, "Let me know if you can hook me up with some of those drugs your mom had. That would be cool."

I fumed inside, felt my face burn beat red. These people thought I was a drug dealer? I crumpled the note, stood up, saw a girl in front of me. She had long perfectly straightened chestnut hair that matched her brown eyes as well as her lip liner. She stood with one hand on her hip and flashed a huge smile at me.

"Hi, Emily. I'm Cameron, class vice president. Welcome to campus. Come on, I'll walk with you to the next class. Where are you going?"

I pulled my schedule from my pocket. "E9, Biology," I said.

"Oh, great. I'm in E11. I'll show you the way."

As much as I wanted to believe she was a really nice person, I felt suspicious. It wasn't that tough to find a class with the huge bold letters in alphabetical order on the side of every building. When we entered the bustling hallway, her cheery little smile morphed into the person I suspected.

"Okay, let's get this straight." She shoved my shoulder, blocking my path. "I don't think I'm going to like you. I'll play nice in front of the teachers and stuff, but outside of class, stay away from my friends, you hear? If I catch you flirting with one of my boys, or chatting it up with one of my girls, you are going to be so sorry you ever stepped onto this campus. I saw Hector talk to you, and guess what? He's one of mine, NOT one of yours. Steer clear." She shoved me on the other shoulder, turned around, and walked toward a group of girls with a look frighteningly similar to Cameron—the darkly lined lips, faded jeans, short tops that showed off either a tattoo along their back or a belly button ring in front.

I stood there in shock before I realized they were all looking at me and laughing. Standing there like an idiot would not help me, so I put on the most non-threatening, yet still confident look I could manage and looked to where I had to go for my next class. Unfortunately, I had to walk past them, and they were clearly in no hurry to get to class on time. Intimidating me with their bewitched glares and cocky smiles was their only care, which they did quite well. I felt every eye on me, heard every comment—"druggie," "jail slut," "white trash," "ugly," "think you're so cool and you're so not."

It was hard to keep my head up, to walk at the same steady pace, to not let them see how their words hurt, to not cry. I didn't think anyone my age ever read a newspaper anymore, but obviously someone had, maybe a parent, and spread the news about my mom. I kept my eyes straight ahead and was so glad to see the letter E on the side of the next building. I stepped up my pace to reach the safe doorway of E9 and entered, relieved to be in a classroom where no one could be openly mean. But instead of noticing a nice teacher, I was greeted by a tall young police officer. He stood next to one of the desks at the door, arms crossed, no smile, clearly not visiting for a friendly talk.

"Student ID?" he said to the girl in front of me. She opened her backpack, he reached in. "Thank you, you can have a seat."

He looked at me, same stern expression, nodded his head. "Student ID?"

I handed him the temporary card Mrs. Beam gave me with my schedule.

"We need to check your bag," he said.

"Oh, sure, here." I handed him my backpack, wondering if this was a routine thing at this school.

He reached his hand in, pulled out my binder, which was all I had in it aside from my dead cell phone, two pencils, and a pen. "Can you explain this?" he said. He held up a small, plastic bag containing what looked like marijuana.

"That isn't mine." My heart felt like it might jump out of my chest. I wanted to throw up. How could that have gotten in my backpack? And why would anyone believe me, the daughter of the drug dealer? I guessed that was how I would feel the presence of my mom at her alma mater.

"Well, it's in your possession," he said. "That's about all the evidence I need. Come with me."

"But it's not mine. Someone planted it there. I've never touched that stuff."

"Okay, well, you need to come with me anyway, darling." He pulled out handcuffs. "We can use these if you'd like, or you can come willingly."

I hated this place so much, hated that he called me darling. Yuck. Maybe he would arrest me and put me in jail. That had to be better. I couldn't hold back the tears now. They poured out of my eyes like little runaways, dying to escape the prison of my lower lids. I walked next to him, my head down now. I didn't care about trying to look cool and confident. I walked outside of the room I thought was safe, into the bustle of students who continued to stare at me, the loser, walking in shame with a police officer. For some reason, I thought of Grandma's words from the other night, "Blessed are the poor in spirit." I hoped she'd be right someday.

# 15

My only previous memory of being in a principal's office was in elementary school when I got a "Caught Being Good" award for letting Ricky Wheeler have my Popsicle on Fun Run Day after he dropped his. I was told to bring my award certificate to the office where Principal Ashby would let me pick a prize from the treasure box in her office. Even then I was scared to death to enter. I figured that office was where all the bad stuff went down. It was where Kimi Garnett got suspended for kicking Ashton Jones in the face and calling him a lame-o. She'd been practicing her karate kicks all day, telling everyone she'd just started classes and was going to be a black belt. Ashton made the mistake of laughing at her.

The principal's office was also where parents went to talk about important things, or where teachers sometimes went with angry or sad looks on their faces. So I entered Principal Ashby's office quickly, my head down, eyes on the treasure chest, and grabbed the first thing my hand touched, a can of playdough. Then I said thank you and scurried back out.

I knew there was no treasure box today, and I knew I wouldn't be in and out quickly, but I was so thankful when Mrs. Beam entered the office. She rushed in, heels clanking the tile floor with short, brisk steps.

"What happened? What's going on muchacha?" she said to me. Though she looked a little angry, I mostly saw concern in her eyes. I felt like I could trust her.

"They found marijuana in my backpack. Maybe you hear this all the time, but I promise it isn't mine. I have no idea how it got there."

She stared into my eyes, like she was a truth detector scanning for lies. "Okay, well, we'll have to see what Mr. Solomon says, right Deputy Harker?"

"Yes Ma'am," the deputy responded. "He will be the one to decide what to do. If the school wants to press charges, it's a Class 2 Petty Offense for possessing the marijuana, giving you a fine and court costs. If you're accused of selling, the penalty could be severe, possibly jail.

My head spun. Shock, anger, fear whirled around inside me like a fierce tornado. This day really had turned out to be one in which I felt closer to Mom, possibly as close as being in jail with her. How had my life become such a mess? How did I suddenly fit the image of bad girl?

The look on Mr. Solomon's face when he appeared confirmed my fear of principals. He sported two angry wrinkles between thick dark eyebrows, and his eyes looked as though they hadn't shut for sleep in weeks.

Mrs. Beam must have seen right through me. She rested her hand lightly on my shoulder and quietly said, "Okay, muchacha, chin up, he's not as scary as he looks."

Mr. Solomon's office, however, was unfriendly. The walls were an odd golden yellow, probably a popular color in the 1970s when the school was built. The pictures on the wall also hinted of days gone by—oil paintings, one of a vase of flowers, another of a mountain scene with a deer in the foreground, framed in ornate gold that tried to look elegant, but instead achieved tacky. My only hope hung on the picture framed in bright red plastic on his desk, angled just enough in my direction to see the words "I Love You, Grandpa" in crayon above a blue handprint about the size of a five-year-old. If his grandkid loved him, maybe he had a heart.

Mrs. Beam and I sat in the only two chairs in front of his desk, while Deputy Harker stood behind us.

"So, Miss Greene, this was in your backpack." Mr. Solomon pushed the clear plastic bag of marijuana at me the way people push coins across a poker table.

Did he want me to take it? Examine it? I stared at it, then looked him straight in the eyes and said, "That isn't mine."

He stared back at me, right into my eyes. I knew he was expecting me to look away, be afraid. Lucky for many a staring contest with Jared, I didn't even blink.

"Well, unfortunately," Mr. Solomon said, "it's your word against the police and me. We have a very strict policy on drugs here, with no grace. You get caught, you're suspended, three days, and if you're suspected of dealing, you're expelled, and if we file charges, you have to go to trial. The suspension is bad enough for now. It'll be on your records though, so keep that in mind when you apply to college, if you plan to go to college. That obviously isn't the plan for some."

Mr. Solomon paused as if waiting for an answer. Of course I was planning on college. Had he seen my grades from my old school? I wasn't perfect, but I wasn't dropout material either. I wanted to yell that at him, along with a bunch of other stuff, like names and bad words, but my perpetual goodie-good desire to please stopped me. I was too scared to buck his authority and have him hate me, even though he seemed to anyway. So I said nothing, refused to give him the satisfaction of knowing my plans for the future. He didn't deserve to know me better. Like Cigarette Jerk, he didn't know my story.

Unfortunately, as I sat there in those quiet seconds while he waited for me to do or say something, I thought of Mom. I wished she was there to help me. A tear began to well up in my eyes. *No Emily, do not do it! Do not cry!* Too late. The tears escaped, ran amuck down my cheek.

"Mr. Solomon," Mrs. Beam started in. "Please keep in mind this is Emily's first day. She has very high marks and comments from her previous school, a model student in behavior and performance. I think we can keep the suspension off her permanent record. She didn't even have a full day of school today, so we can easily move her enrollment date up three days and not count today as her first day. We don't need to make this so difficult. Come on, Solomon, you're better than this."

I was impressed with her boldness to talk to him like that in front of me. She gave him that look I only see people give each other when they know each other well, like the way Jared does when he calls me out on something with a single look. It's enough to stop me dead in my tracks when I'm annoying him or doing something stupid.

Mr. Solomon sighed, rubbed his hand on his brow, then sat back in his chair, arms folded.

"Miss Greene, I'm going to suspend you because it's a rule."

Mrs. Beam stood up, "Hay Dios Mio, Solomon, de verdad?"

The little bit of Spanish I knew told me that meant, Oh my God, Solomon, really?

Mrs. Beam rested her hands on her hips and glared at him. This appeared to be a definite quick draw of wills.

"But," Mr. Solomon continued, glaring back at Mrs. Beam, "since Mrs. Beam is your counselor, and is willing and able to correct your enrollment date, we won't add this to your permanent record," he paused and then added, "this time. Next time will be a different story. I suggest you do whatever it takes to stay out of trouble and avoid hanging out with the wrong crowd."

I wanted to explain that the "crowd" he meant was not my crowd anyway. That crowd consisted of the people who just planted drugs in my backpack. They wouldn't have done that if

I was one of them. So his advice to stay away from certain students wasn't real helpful. But all I wanted now was to be out of his office. Mr. Solomon didn't care about my social problems. He simply followed the written rules in his handbook, whether they actually helped anyone or not.

As much as I didn't have any positive feelings for the office manager, she managed to provide a small amount of happiness when she came through Mr. Solomon's door to tell me my freedom from his wrath had arrived.

"Mr. Solomon, Emily's grandmother, Carol Greene, is here. Should I send her in?"

Mr. Solomon looked at his watch. "Actually, Mrs. Beam, can you take Emily and speak to her grandmother? I'm late for a meeting at the district office."

"Sí, no problem," she responded as she promptly stood up, seeming as thrilled to escape as me.

I was so glad to be out of there. But when I saw Grandma, I wondered if maybe Mr. Solomon's office was a better place to be. Grandma stood out in the worst possible way. She wore bright orange pants that probably came with a matching jacket like the blue ones she wore to our house when we met her. But these pants were topped with the oversized tie-dye T-shirt she wore to bed. A shiny, silver cross, about the size of my hand, hung from a long leather band around her neck.

She saw me immediately and spoke loud and clear from across the room, "Oh Emily, my dear. We need to pray about this." She grabbed my hand, held it tight, placed the cross on top of my hand. I felt every eye in the office stare at me, and saw two girls laugh who sat on a bench behind Grandma.

"Dear Heavenly Father," she began. She whispered now, but I felt like she was shouting.

"Uh, Grandma, can we maybe do this in the car or at home?" I couldn't take any more stares. She completely ignored me.

"We praise you for your mighty works and the discipline of

your hand when we stray. We ask that you resolve any wrongs that have been committed here in this—"

"Grandma! Please stop! Your prayers aren't helping me!"

I saw the laughing girls open their mouths and stare wide-eyed at each other. The bustle of the room was now a stale, awkward silence. If people weren't paying attention before, they were now. I so wished I could be swallowed into the earth and disappear. That was the miracle of God I wanted now.

I looked at Grandma, and for the first time, she actually looked angry at me. Mrs. Beam interrupted the uncomfortable silence, again making me so glad she was there.

"Mrs. Greene, I'm Emily's counselor." She reached her hand out to shake Grandma's. "I think Emily's had a bit of a rough afternoon. How beautiful of you to say a prayer. We could use more of that around here."

I was shocked she didn't act like my grandmother was crazy, and now I felt horrible for yelling at Grandma, even though she had been a bit dramatic and was completely embarrassing me. Here I was hoping she would disappear, insulting her prayers, while she was the one positive thing besides Mrs. Beam in the entire room. Why did I care about impressing all those idiots who were laughing at me?

"Let's go talk in private for a minute," Mrs. Beam said.

We followed her, past the gawkers, the silent judgers, the laughers, and then sat down in her office.

"So, I'm sure you're wondering why you were called to pick up Emily," Mrs. Beam began.

"Yes, I am very concerned," Grandma said. I saw she was holding a rock, squeezing it between her palms, and her eyes looked weary, absent of their normal glimmer and cheer.

"So, marijuana was found in Emily's backpack."

Grandma gasped, but Mrs. Beam continued right away.

"I think I believe Emily when she says the marijuana isn't hers, but when we find something in someone's possession, we have to act. Emily, my advice to you is to be extra careful when you return to school. If you have your backpack out of your sight, it's easy for someone to slip something in it. My guess is some students heard the police were on campus, so they possibly chose to hide their drugs in your bag."

I thought about all the moments that could have happened. In English class, I had my backpack behind me, on the floor. Who sat behind me? That cute blonde girl, sort of a clone of Cameron, or maybe Hector, when he gave me the note, he could have slipped it in the backpack, or maybe one of Cameron's friends when she shoved me and talked to me with "her girls" behind me.

"I'll be careful," I said, "but it seems unfair that I'm in trouble and no one else has been questioned. What am I supposed to do, keep my backpack on my lap in class? Hold it in front of me when I walk? Whoever put it in there knew how to do it without getting caught. They probably do this all the time."

"I agree with you, Emily, believe me. It makes me angry too. I don't have the best answers, but I would do whatever you can to guard your things."

I stared speechless at her after that. I knew she didn't think her advice was worthwhile. I knew she didn't have any solutions to this problem. I figured I should be glad that at least she was on my side.

Grandma extended her hand for Mrs. Beam's, "God bless you, dear. I can tell you're a good egg. Please keep an eye out for my Emily when she comes back, okay?"

"Absolutely, Mrs. Greene, will do." She put her hand on top of Grandma's and held it there.

Grandma looked like she might cry, her eyes watery, her mouth quivering a little. She stood up and said, "Okay, Emily, let's go."

I followed Grandma to the door, but then stopped and turned around before we left. "Thank you, Mrs. Beam."

"You're welcome, Emily. See you soon." She gave me a warm smile, one that told me she really did believe in me. Maybe I was finally getting a small blessing as one of those "poor in spirit" types.

# -16-

When I got home, all I could think about was the unfairness of my life. I sat on the couch in front of the television, flipped channels until I found repeats of a show I sometimes watched, "Star Dancers." I was definitely not a dancer, even though I did take a year of ballet classes when I was six. I wanted to keep going with it, but Mom said we didn't have the money to continue anymore. I got the chance to try gymnastics when I turned seven, when Mom said she could afford it, but after a month, she said we couldn't, so I quit that too. The same cycle continued for an art class, swim lessons, and tennis. So, to see someone dance so beautifully, after years of dedicated training and sacrifice, sort of wowed me.

At the beginning of each episode, the dancers who were competing had ten seconds to say all they could about themselves. Today, the dancer, named Jo Desmani, said, "I attend Bardley College, I have three brothers, I love cake, I like rap music, my dog is a German shepherd."

I got up from the television, went into the bathroom, stared in the mirror. "My mom is in jail, I'm suspended for marijuana possession, I hate my new high school filled with jerks and snobs, I don't know my father, I hope to be a writer, but my life sucks too much." I figured that was an accurate ten-second biography of my life.

I heard a tap on the bathroom door. "Emily, can I talk to you for a few minutes?" I so did not want to talk to Grandma, hear her nature stories and her lectures and her Bible verses and her tea bag quotes. But I couldn't really say no. What else could I say I was doing? It was either get it over with, or know it would come later. I opened the door.

"What, Grandma." That came out ruder than I meant it to, but I couldn't control my anger.

"Come on, let's sit down on the porch, shall we? There's a nice breeze outside."

I felt both annoyed and pleased with her patience. I never got away with speaking like that to Mom. Maybe Mom spoke to her that way as a kid, so she was used to it. Maybe that explained why Mom was so messed up; Grandma didn't command her respect, so Mom got away with too much.

We sat on the front porch in two wicker chairs stuffed with pillows. Dust and dirt clung to them, probably from the wind that kicked up most nights. Aside from a large tree, dust and dirt was also my current view.

"So, my yard isn't perfect, Emily, but if you look at it the right way, it's actually quite beautiful," she said.

*Here goes,* I thought, *Grandma's thoughts on dirt and sticks again.*

"I know people call me Crazy Carol."

Her switch in topics surprised me. Plus, how horrible that she knew people called her that.

"I'm okay with them calling me crazy. They see me gathering sticks and leaves and branches and rocks, sometimes talking to them. But they don't really know me, Emily. They don't know my life, why I collect things they might walk right by. So, actually, the crazier they think I am, the more stuff I intend to collect. Because with each simple thing I gather, I think of the beauty in it, the good in it. That dirt out there may not look as pretty as green grass, but God still created it. Each little thing he made has a purpose, even those people who might be rude to me and call me crazy. He will make good out of that somehow. He promises that when he says all things will work together for the good of those who love him."

I liked the thought of what she was saying, but I still didn't really believe her.

"I wish I didn't care what other people thought," I said. "I don't know how to do that."

Grandma's smile showed me she understood that feeling. She stood up, walked down the porch steps to her dirt yard. "I'll be right back," she said.

I watched her short careful steps, the dirt that sputtered behind her heels, the way she scoured every inch of dirt with her eyes. The bright orange pants, the tie-dye shirt, were no longer an embarrassment. She was the only bright spot in the yard.

"Aha! Here it is!" She spun around, holding a tiny something in her hand. For the first time, I saw her jog. She shuffled up the steps, set a tiny white pebble, dull and plain, on my leg. Then she stood back, an even brighter smile on her face, as though I just received a new car and should get up and thank her for the gift.

"Uh, thank you?" I said, unclear about what else to say. I picked up the pebble and rolled it between my fingers. I looked closer at it, but still saw a boring stone.

"Oh, you don't need to thank me," she said. She sat back down in her chair. "But you can thank the one who made it, the one who made that little rock to remind you of your true value."

I definitely didn't know how to respond to that, and though I wanted to know what she meant, I didn't want to hear how I was at all similar to an insignificant pebble. But my curiosity, and possibly the desire to laugh, got the best of me. "I'm not sure a rock is the thing I hoped reminded me of my worth, Grandma."

"Well, sounds like I need to explain." She winked at me.

I took a deep breath and tried to be patient.

Grandma continued, "So in the Bible, there are several verses about rocks. One of them is from 1 Peter 2:4. It says Jesus is the "living stone, rejected by humans, but chosen by God and precious to him." She stopped and smiled. If she was done with her explanation, I was very disappointed. This didn't strike me as interesting or relatable to me in any way.

"Okay, I know I need to explain more." Her eyes lit up as she continued. "Jesus, the living son of God, was rejected by many. But he is precious to God. When we are treated badly, rejected by people, we are also still precious to God, just like Jesus is. We aren't worthless, insignificant stones. We are valuable."

I liked what she was trying to tell me, but I didn't feel her excitement at all. I didn't really believe it.

"I know I must sound crazy to you, Emily. Like I said, I've been told that before, from people in this town, your mom, whoever. But I've also been told by some that they agree, they understand, or that they'll think about it. I hope you'll be one of them. I hope you'll see that you are like this little stone. You might think others see you as insignificant, but you're not.

Until now, everything I knew about religion or God or Jesus seemed negative to me.

"Mom says God can't be real, says if he is, why doesn't he make her life better?"

Grandma nodded her head, like she'd heard that before. "That's what some people think when everything doesn't turn out how they want, when they want. I thought that for a while. But God isn't a magic genie, and some of the things we want would actually be horrible for us."

"So, was Mom happy as a kid?"

"Well, yes, up until she was about your age. I think all the moving we did might have gotten to her. She never had a chance to feel settled. Once we did adjust to a new place, her dad ended up moving to a new military base. It was a bit rough on her."

I could understand that. I guess she went through what I was going through over and over. It sucked going to a new school, not knowing anyone, feeling awkward. But at least she had her parents.

"What do you know about my dad?" I asked. No point in waiting on that question. I'd wanted an answer about him since my mom last told me not to ask anymore. I think I was six.

"Your dad?" She looked surprised, but not angry like Mom always did when I asked that question. "Well, he was a nice boy, really loved your mom. But he also had ambitions and was quite smart. He had a scholarship to some college on the east coast, don't remember which one, but he decided to go. The week before he was to leave he learned your mom was pregnant. He left, told her he'd be back, that he'd get a good education so he could take care of her. But his leaving crushed your mom. She took it the wrong way, felt like he was putting his life before hers."

"Well, maybe he was, but for a good reason, an education. She really didn't understand that?" I was shocked. She always told me to pursue my dreams, my education, that school came first. "Mom said he left because he wanted nothing to do with us, said he refused to help her or support us."

Grandma's happy face disappeared. She picked up the pebble I'd set on the arm of my chair, fiddled with it between her fingers, took a deep breath, stared into my eyes with teary ones of her own.

"I hate to be the one to tell you this, Emily, but that is not the truth." She hesitated, as if she didn't know how to continue.

"So, what is the truth?" I asked, a little afraid to hear it.

"Your father sent letters to your mom while he was away. She read some, then threw them out. She never told me what was in the letters, but since she seemed so angry, I figured he wasn't being real nice. One summer after your mom left here to be on her own with you, he knocked on the door, asked where she was. I was kind of rude to him, told him she'd left, was happy to be without him. He was crushed. He said he'd been trying to get in touch with her, but she never responded to him. He started crying right here on my porch. I'd never thought that boy had a tear in his body, always seemed so confident and happy."

What was she saying? He tried to find us? He actually cared about us?

"Are you kidding me?" I jumped up from my seat, unable to sit still, paced back and forth, then faced Grandma again as I unleashed all my frustration. "What was her problem? Why would she ignore him? Why would she lie to me? She's such a fake about everything! She lies about her problem with drugs; she lies about my father. The mom I thought was amazing is a selfish liar!"

I was sobbing, like my father surely did on that very same porch, possibly in the very same chair, hurt by the very same person.

"I'm so sorry to tell you this, Emily. I didn't want to make you angry, but I also can't lie to you."

"I'm not mad at you. I'm glad you told me the truth. But I don't understand any part of my life right now. It's all so messed up." I cried like I did the day Mom went to jail. I cried so hard it hurt my stomach and I felt like I couldn't get a breath.

Grandma held me in her arms, never told me to stop crying, told me to let it all out. I stared at the pebble as my tears lessened. I remembered what Grandma said, but I didn't know how my stupid life could have any purpose, how I could be valuable, or how any of this could happen if there was a God who loved me.

# –17–

All that talk about my dad made me think of Richard. Since I thought my father didn't want anything to do with me, I used to wish Richard might become the father I didn't have. But I figured out pretty quickly that having no father would be better than having him.

I realized this the day our air conditioning stopped working, only a few months after Richard moved in with us. It was during a summer heat wave. I sat at the kitchen table with a bowl of Cheerios and Richard, who hunched over his phone and squinted at the screen. At 7:30 in the morning it already felt like the middle of a hot afternoon in our house.

I tried to think of something to say, something a dad might want to talk about. "Any good news stories today?" I'd heard him report the events of the day to my mom whenever he read his news app. I didn't really have any interest in the news, but it was better than listening to Mom talk to the air conditioning control panel, which clearly wasn't making the air conditioner come on.

He shuffled his feet under the table, while I continued to watch Mom push the buttons of the panel more aggressively. Then he finally said, "What did you say?" His eyes squinted at me and he shook his head, clearly annoyed that I had disturbed his quiet time.

"I asked if there are any good news stories today."

"Uh, no, not that you'd care about."

So much for that conversation. I bit into some cereal at the same time Mom announced, "The AC is dead."

Richard's hand slammed the table. My bowl bounced up, splashing milk over the sides, and my orange juice glass teetered sideways. I tried to grab it, but instead knocked it as it spilled over the edge of the table. Richard jumped up, but not quick enough to avoid juice spilling across his pants.

His red face scrunched into pure outrage. My heart beat like it did in a race, but not because of exhaustion.

"Dammit, Emily! What the hell are you doing? Get a towel!" he snapped.

I jumped up, banged my hip on the edge of the table, and almost slipped in the puddle of juice. I grabbed a towel on the kitchen counter and ran to clean up the mess. I reached for the floor, but Richard grabbed my wrist.

"Don't clean up the floor first! Get the table! Were you going to wipe the dirty floor and then put it on the table? That's plain stupid. Dammit, where is your brain?"

I tried to pull my wrist away, but he clamped down harder. I felt myself begin to cry. He was hurting me, and I didn't understand why.

"Richard, let her go. I'll clean it up." Mom said timidly.

He let go of me and whipped around to face her. "What? Are you arguing with how I handle this? She's old enough to clean up her own mess. You need to call someone to come fix the air conditioner. I'm not going to sit in this boiling house while you're off enjoying your air conditioned hospital!"

I wished Jared were home. He'd been away at basketball camp. He would have stopped Richard. He would have helped Mom. But he wasn't home, and Richard was a moving wrecking ball. My mom stood for a second, maybe two, probably trying to figure out what the heck was wrong with this lunatic in her house. I saw her start to speak, her lips barely cracked open, before he shoved his hands into her and pushed her like she was an opponent on a football field. She fell backward, into the wall where the stupid air conditioning control panel had ruined our morning.

"Mom!" I left the towel on the floor, right where Richard didn't want it, and ran to her. I put my hand on her head and helped her get her balance. She looked at me with wide eyes, took short, fast breaths, gripped my arm with one hand and held my shoulder with the other, begging me without words to be her strength, but once she looked at Richard, she quickly stood up straight and smiled the phoniest smile ever.

"I'm okay, honey. I'm fine. Let me just make that call, okay?"

Richard said nothing. He didn't ask her if she was okay. He didn't tell her he was sorry. He did nothing but smile that sick smile of his, nod his head, and walk past us down the hall.

The air conditioner got fixed, but not with any help from Richard. Mom ended up having to switch shifts with someone so she could be home for the repair man. Richard claimed he couldn't stay because he had a meeting. I knew he was lying. He had already said he planned to be at home. But no one was going to argue with him. We had been too afraid.

I wished now I could go back to that day. I'd gladly argue with him. In my mind, he was one huge wimp, running from cops, letting his fiancée sit in jail, abandoning his kid. I wasn't scared of losers like him, and I couldn't wait to let him know it.

# 18

On day two of my three-day suspension I decided I needed to visit Mom again. I didn't know how I'd get there, but I had to find a way. It was times like this that made me wish I had my driver's license.

"I've gotta see Mom," I told Jared after nudging him awake at seven in the morning.

He rubbed his eyes, tried to focus them. "I can take you this weekend if you want," he said.

"Thanks, that would be great, but I actually want to go today. I have nothing else to do but sit here and feel angry at her. I don't know if I can wait until the weekend. I need to find out why she's been lying to me." I knew that sounded selfish, but I felt like I might explode. Actually, I had every intention of exploding, but I only wanted to do so at her, not anyone else who might get caught in the crossfire of my anger because she wasn't around.

"I'd be happy to ditch school, say I'm sick or something, but I have that meeting with the basketball coach to see if I can get on the team for offseason and summer league. Can you ask your grandma to take you?"

I considered that for a moment, but then remembered how she drove. It was a little scary the way she sped up real fast and then slammed on the breaks at either a stop sign or something she saw that interested her. "I guess I could ask her, but I'm fearful of my life in her car. On the way home from school the day of my suspension she actually stopped in the middle of the road to pick up a stray flower petal that blew across her windshield."

Jared laughed, "Oh man, that's hilarious, sorry." He kept laughing.

His laugh always made me laugh too. "Okay, so I know it's funny, but I hope you can survive on your own for a while because if she drives like that all the way to the jail, it will take us about a week to get there. Or, we'll get hit by someone and you'll have the rest of your life on your own."

He laughed even more now, clearly not taking my plea seriously. "I think you'll be okay. She's been driving that way for years obviously, and she's still here. It will probably be annoying, but I think she'll keep you safe. Plus, I think God has an extra eye out for her with all that praying she does."

I was a little surprised to hear him say this. "You think her prayers are helping her? You really believe that?" I asked.

"Well, I don't know. My mom prayed a lot, used to pray with me each night."

"Not to be mean or anything, Jared, but those prayers didn't seem to work out so well for her."

He stayed quiet for a bit, then said, "You know, I actually think her prayers might have worked. She never really prayed for a cure for her cancer. She always prayed for me, that I would be safe, that what was meant to be would be. I prayed for her to stop hurting. So maybe taking her to heaven is how she finally felt better, I don't know. And as for me, I have been taken care of, even though things haven't been easy."

"Wow, listen to you preach it. I didn't know you believed in God. You don't ever talk about it."

"I guess that's because I sometimes have doubts. There's a

lot of stuff I don't understand. But deep down, I think God is there. Maybe because my mom believed it, so I want to believe it."

That made sense. I didn't believe because my mom didn't believe. So, I could see how he might follow what he learned from his mom.

"Okay, so you really think I can survive a drive with Crazy Carol?"

"Yes, I really think you can. Go ask her."

While Jared managed to convince me to ask, I didn't get the answer I had hoped.

"Emily, I'm sorry. I don't think it's a good idea to go visit your mom right now. You were pretty upset the last time you went. Maybe you should wait a couple weeks."

I couldn't believe she said this. How would waiting make it any better? Visiting Mom and being disappointed was better than not seeing her at all. I needed answers. I needed to find out why she had kept me from knowing my dad and tell her to stop lying to me.

"Grandma, I don't need to wait. I need to talk to her. Don't tell me what's good for me when you hardly even know me."

My words drained any trace of happiness from her face. Her eyes stared straight into mine like she was trying to figure out how I could be so mean. I sort of wished she would yell at me so we could at least be equally cruel. But instead, she sadly said, "Okay dear, maybe I don't know you perfectly, but I'm still doing what I think is best since I'm the one taking care of you. So, if that reason isn't good enough, I'll give you another one. My car isn't running so well. I'm not sure it will make it all the way to your mom and back. I'll schedule a day to get it looked at, and we can go after that."

She had me there, both in the calm response I didn't deserve and the car excuse. I stood there and said nothing as she walked into the kitchen.

"Sounds like that went well," Jared said when I walked past his room.

I rolled my eyes and sighed. "Yep, perfect."

I leaned against his doorway while he sat on the floor, tying his shoes. "Sorry I can't help, Em. I can take you on the weekend though. That's sooner than Grandma will take you, and it's only two days away."

"Yeah, I know. No big deal. Thanks, Jared."

He grabbed my foot gently. "Maybe you should try these feet out today. Go for a run or something. Might make you feel better as long as your ankle is okay. And maybe we can watch something dumb on TV tonight when I get back, or you can sing along while I play guitar. You can even pick the songs."

That got a smile out of me, which is of course why he said all that.

"Sounds good," I said.

He smiled back and I closed my eyes, actually wishing I could go to school with him. That sounded better than staying in this house where I had nothing to do but think. Thinking was like torture. I thought about Jared's advice to go for a run, and decided he was probably right. A run usually worked to clear my thoughts.

I grabbed my shoes from my room, slid them onto my feet, and imagined them springing across the dirt path down Grandma's driveway, onto the street where I would run away from here for a while. I breezed down the hall and waved to Jared, who sat at the table eating a bowl of cereal. "Good luck with basketball," I said.

"Thanks, I hope your run is good."

Before I opened the door to escape, Grandma stopped me, handed me a ribbon with numbers written in sharpie. "Here, put this around your wrist. I know your phone isn't working and assume you don't know my number, so this way you have it until you remember it. I'll try to figure out how to pay for a phone plan eventually, but for now, at least you can reach me if something happens."

She tied the ribbon loosely around my wrist, and as much as I wanted to pull my hand away in protest of her protectiveness, I couldn't do it as she gently held my hand, smiled warmly, and said, "Have a nice run, dear."

I walked out the door, feeling a little like a dog with an identification tag in case I got lost. The cool morning air and clear skies made me forget about that quickly; it was my favorite kind of day for a run. I eagerly took my first few strides, excited for the feeling of my feet springing from the ground. But after a few more steps at only a slow jog, my dream of carefree running escaped me. I wished I could blame it on my ankle, but it felt fine. The rest of my body was the problem. My legs felt like huge weights attached to my hips. My feet pounded hard on the cement, no spring in them at all. The cool air didn't help. I sucked it in with deep breaths, my heart already pumping too fast.

What was wrong with me? Why couldn't I enjoy this? Why couldn't I feel free and light? The trees that lined the street reminded me of home, where I would normally run under tall branches that formed a safe canopy of shade and dropped leaves that crunched beneath my feet. But these trees seemed to taunt me, their branches low, causing me to duck under them, their leaves dancing to music I couldn't hear. After maybe five minutes, I had to stop. I bent over, my hands on my knees, my breath heavy.

I heard a car coming from behind, and then saw it slow down beside me.

"Hey girl, can I give you a ride? You don't seem to have much luck on your own two feet around here."

I looked up to see Ginny behind the wheel, and a man with a balding scalp and thick glasses in the passenger seat.

"No, I'm fine, just more out of shape than I thought. Running feels like torture today."

"Ha! Welcome to my world. Running is torture every day."

That was a comment I heard from most people. Now I could relate. "I thought you couldn't drive yet," I said.

"She can't," the man immediately responded. "She insists on driving on this road to school every morning so she can practice. Once we hit the main road, she's back in the passenger seat. Otherwise, she'd never make it to school alive."

"Wow, thanks for the encouragement, Dad."

"Any time sweetheart. So is this the Emily I've been hearing about?"

I wasn't sure if I should say yes. The things he might have heard could be bad. Luckily, Ginny answered for me.

"Yes, it is. The awesome Emily Greene. One of the few good things to happen to this town in my lifetime."

"Aw, thanks Ginny."

"Well, it's a pleasure to meet you, Emily. Are you sure you don't want a ride?"

"No, a walk will do me good. I'm heading back now, so it's not too far, but thank you."

"Okay, well, can I call you when I get to school? I'm early, so I'll be bored and alone until class starts," Ginny said.

"Sure, that would be great. But you need to call my grandma's home phone since my phone isn't working."

"Okay, sure, what's the number?"

I laughed to myself as I lifted my wrist and held it toward Ginny so she could see the numbers on my newest fashion accessory.

"Oh, wow, that's cute." She winked at me, smiled, and tapped the digits into her phone. "Talk to you soon." She pulled away with a jolt of the car and a screech of the tires.

I laughed and heard her dad yell, "Geez Ginny, lighten up those feet, would you?"

He could have been saying that to me as well. Lighten up those feet, Emily. Stop plodding along on those big blocks of lead. But I kept trudging along, back up that street I never escaped. I grabbed a leaf from a branch that hung from a tree in front of me. It was smooth and damp. I rubbed it between my fingers, thought of bringing it home to give to Grandma. But I tossed it onto the ground instead. She didn't need another leaf, and I didn't need one of her stories. I needed my mom.

# 19

I picked up my pace a little after Ginny drove away, alternating between jogs and walks so I could get home in time for her phone call. I used every last bit of energy to trudge up Grandma's porch steps, opened the front door and panted heavily with my hands on my knees as the phone rang.

"Oh man, I have to move again," I said between breaths as I jogged to the phone.

"Hey speed demon, are you home?" Ginny asked after I said hello.

"Yes, I just made it, but barely. I think I might die."

"Okay, we really should run together. That's how I always feel. But are you okay? I mean, you looked kind of sad out there, which again is how I always look when I run, but I'm thinking that isn't your problem. Your life basically sucks right now."

I so appreciated Ginny's blunt honesty. She never tried to tell me to look on the bright side or that things would get better. I didn't need that right now.

"Hold on one sec." I set the phone down on the kitchen counter and walked into the living room, "Grandma? Are you here?" I stopped at the hallway and yelled again, "Grandma?" I jogged back to the phone. "Okay, sorry, I wanted to make sure I had some privacy. Grandma's probably outside collecting things."

Ginny laughed, "Oh, well, based on what I saw when I was there, she gathers a lot, so hopefully you have some time. Go for it, tell me what's going on."

"Well, I really want to see my mom, which may seem crazy based on how bad she made me feel last time, but my grandma told me some things about my dad that I really want to clear up with her, and even though I'm mad at her, I miss her."

"That's completely understandable. So, why don't you go?"

"Unless I walk, I have no way to get there. My grandmother wants me to wait awhile before I see her again, and Jared has some basketball meeting."

"So, how about me?"

I was pretty sure she knew the answer to that. "Um, you don't have a license, remember? And I'm not going to let your parents take me. That would be so embarrassing."

"Okay, it's not embarrassing. They know about your mom, and they don't think badly of you. They feel bad for you. But I didn't offer them. I'm offering me. I've had enough practice to get you there safely."

"Ginny, are you crazy? If you get pulled over, you're toast."

"I'll just say I forgot my license. I can talk my way out of it. Last month Chris and I drove an hour to go watch his uncle's cow give birth. A cop drove right past me and didn't stop. There would be no reason to pull me over if I'm driving safe."

I loved her confidence, and the fact that her last adventure was to watch the birth of a calf. But it still seemed unnecessary. "Ginny, I don't know. That seems way too risky. Why would you want to do that?"

"Um, because it's fun. And I have nothing else to do after school but sit in my empty house since my parents are both working late. And it helps you. Are those good enough reasons?"

"If both your parents are at work, how are you going to get a car?"

"Because we have a spare key to my mom's car at my house, and I know it's going to be sitting in the hospital parking lot until midnight because that's when she gets off work. We can easily walk to the hospital, get her car, and have it back before she even knows it's gone."

It was as if she'd been planning this all along. The thought of it not only made me feel relieved that I could see Mom, but it sounded kind of fun. I hadn't had fun in a while. "Wow, you have this all figured out."

"Yep, I do. So, yes? I'll see you around noon? I just have to go to the nurse's office after fourth period and tell her I'm not feeling well. She'll call my mom, and my mom will pick me up before her shift starts. Then I'll walk over to your place.

"Wow, you have a lot of experience with planning devious schemes to get out of class."

"Well, I've never ditched class, but I was sick once and had to leave, so I know how it works. Other than that day, I have perfect attendance, so I can afford to skip my afternoon classes today."

"Since you seem to have everything figured out, I almost feel like it's destined for us to go. I see no reason not to."

"All right then, see you in a few hours, bye."

I hung up and felt magically light on my feet again. I wasn't sure how I'd be able to get away from Grandma's watchful eye for the day, but I had time to figure that out. I decided to wait to tell her my plan right before noon so there wouldn't be time for a lot of questions when Ginny arrived.

I managed to find things to do in spite of not having a phone to kill the time. I took a long hot shower, dumped all the clothes from my suitcase to find my favorite comfy jeans, refolded everything neatly and placed it all in neat stacks. Then I wrote in my journal, described how much I missed my mom, how I didn't understand who she was anymore, how I hoped she'd tell me the truth about my father. Thinking I could find out more about him, I tried to connect to the internet on my laptop, but realized Grandma didn't have any technology, so no internet. Finally, with nothing else to do, I decided to explore more of Mom's room. I'd been afraid to do that since anything that reminded me of her made me miss her terribly. But I also wanted to know more about her. It seemed there might be plenty she hadn't told me.

I opened a couple dresser drawers that turned out to be empty, but the third one was heavy, and I had to use both hands to pull it open. It tipped with a thud on the floor once I succeeded. Inside were three rows of colorful mugs, next to several ceramic bowls and containers with lids, vases, and a light blue folder stuffed with papers. I picked up one of the mugs, a bright red one with white hearts. The edges were rounded and the sides had subtle indentations, like thumbprints, pressed between the hearts. I turned it over to see letters engraved on the bottom—LS loves TG. LS—my dad's initials. He made this?

I grabbed another mug, and a dish, and sure enough, each one had either LS or Landon etched in them. Mom always loved different mugs, had way too many crammed into a kitchen cupboard at home. Maybe this was what started that.

When I opened the folder, I found award certificates for Track, Honor Roll, Student of the Month, and under these, a stack of folded papers. I opened them to see handwritten notes, some filling the page, some with only a few lines. They were from my dad, all clearly showing that he adored my mom, that he wasn't sure he wanted to keep running track until she joined and made it worth it, funny little rhymes like a corny limerick that began, "there once was a boy from Pine View who really was in love with you," and my personal favorite, a page filled with lyrics from the song "With or Without You" by U2 along with a note at the bottom that said, "Loved hanging out with you today, listening to your new favorite song over and over.

Here's the words so you can get them right." This made me laugh, remembering the many times Mom would confidently and loudly sing along to songs she liked even if she didn't really know the words.

I was jolted back to reality at the sound of Grandma's tea kettle whistling in the other room. The clock next to the bed brightly displayed that it was 11:45, time to go tell Grandma about my afternoon plans. I took a deep breath. *Act casual, Emily. It's one small lie, not a big deal.*

When I entered the kitchen, Grandma was sipping her tea and reading her Bible. I couldn't look at those pages and tell a blatant lie, so I focused on the steam rising from her cup instead and said, "So, Ginny is coming over for lunch if that's okay."

"Oh, sure it is. Does she like grilled cheese?"

Grandma's kindness made lying to her really difficult. "Um, yes, but she actually wanted to walk to her mom's work to have lunch there. Good cafeteria food, I guess."

"Oh, well that's nice, and that's probably better for you to get out and about anyway. Do you want me to drive you girls there or pick you up after?"

I hadn't thought about that response from her. Time to think quickly.

"Oh, no, that's okay. I think Ginny prefers to walk, and so do I. But thanks anyway."

"Okay, well, I might not be here when you get back. I need to go to the store, and then I was going to go for another little walk myself. It's been a beautiful day to gather pretty stones, sticks, and leaves."

*Oh my, back to leaves again,* I thought.

"Yeah, I saw plenty of them. They're definitely out there today."

Grandma gave me a funny smile, like maybe she sensed my weak attempt to act enthused about leaves, but then responded with her usual sweetness. "Well, maybe I'll find one just for you then."

"Thanks, Grandma," I said, trying to sound more sincere. Luckily, a knock on the door interrupted anymore discussion. "Oh, that must be Ginny." I rushed to the door. "Bye, Grandma! Good luck gathering sticks and stuff!" I shouted, and closed the door before she had time to talk to Ginny.

"Wow, you're certainly in a hurry now," Ginny said.

"Oh, yeah, definitely. Let's go before I chicken out."

Little did I know there was more to fear than I thought.

# –20–

We made it to the hospital pretty quickly, walking at a pace much quicker than my morning run. Ginny found her mom's car, and fortunately no one was around to see us get in.

After about thirty seconds into driving with Ginny, I became aware that the drive might actually be worse than driving with Grandma. First, she battled with the gear shift, then she revved the engine too high after accidentally placing the car in park, then jolted in reverse out of the parking space.

"How much practice have you had driving?" I asked.

"Oh, let's see, aside from that hour drive with Chris I told you about, I've driven to school every morning this week."

It was Wednesday. Ginny said this as if that was all she needed.

As Ginny swerved to avoid a car that cut into her lane, I wondered how we could possibly make it without getting pulled over for reckless driving.

"God help us," I said out loud, actually meaning it more as an actual prayer than a meaningless expression this time.

I spent the rest of the drive mostly holding my breath, gripping the seat of the car, pressing my foot into the floor as if that would help us brake. I had a newfound respect for driver's training and the DMV. I borrowed Ginny's phone to text Jared that Ginny was taking me to see Mom, and that Grandma thought I was simply hanging out at Ginny's house. I figured he might go home and wonder where I was, start looking for me and get Grandma worried.

I knew it was unusual to shout "alleluia" when arriving at jail, but that's what I did the second the front tires entered the parking lot after almost three hours.

"Really? You're that happy to be here?" Ginny asked.

"Yes I am," I said with no intention of explaining my real reason—that we were still alive and soon to be out of the most frightening roller coaster of a car ride. "So, only family is allowed to visit, but you can sit in the waiting room and enjoy the fresh scent of day old coffee and mildew."

"Hmmm, that's a tempting offer. I planned to go with you for moral support, but now I would only be doing it for the tantalizing environment."

"Funny," I laughed, glad that I still could.

I started to open the door, but Ginny's phone rang and Jared's name lit up on her screen. I waited as she picked it up. "Hey Jared, what's up?" She waited for his response, then said, "Sure, here she is." Ginny handed me her phone.

"Hey, everything okay?" I asked him.

"I can't talk long, Em. I'm with my dad. He's paying for gas and doesn't know I'm on the phone with you. He told me to drive him to the house to get stuff he hid there, said his car wouldn't make it and it was important. I don't know what he's up to or why he came to get me, Em, but meet me there if you can. I should be there in a couple hours."

"What? What kind of stuff would be hidden at our house?" I asked, "And why would he need you with him? Does Grandma know? How could she let you go with him?" My head was spinning with panic and questions.

"I didn't see her, Em. He was standing at the edge of her

driveway when I got home from school. He stopped me there and sort of forced this all on me. There's not a whole lot your grandma could do. He's my dad, and she doesn't need to deal with him. He's my problem, not hers. Oh, there he is. I gotta hang up."

"But Jared, wait . . ."

I looked at the phone. He was no longer there.

"What's wrong?" Ginny asked.

"Jared said he's going with Richard. He wants me to meet them at our old house. What is happening?" I felt my breath rising, like I couldn't suck in enough air, worse than my run this morning. "Oh my God, what is going on?"

"Hey, Em, it's okay. Don't panic. From what you've told me about Richard, he's not that smart, and I can drive you there. So, do you want to go now or do you still want to see your mom?"

"Oh, I definitely want to see my mom. She might know what Richard's up to, and we've got enough time to talk to her and still get back to my place in time. I don't even care anymore about how she lied to me about my father. I've gotta find out what she knows about Richard so we can help Jared."

"Okay, well, go on then, and don't stress. We've got this."

I wanted to hug her, but I didn't have time. I needed to be quick.

I was glad I had been to visit Mom once already. I knew the routine of going through security, signing in, waiting for her to arrive, which all seemed torturously long. But what I didn't expect was the way Mom looked and acted this time.

When I arrived inside the visitors' area, I saw my mom ten pounds lighter, hands shaking, skin drab, and eyes weepy.

Her mood was just as bad. "Nice of you to finally visit," she said, her arms crossed tight.

I wasn't sure how to respond. Was I supposed to come more often? Did she have any idea how difficult it was to get there? I felt like I'd been punched in the gut.

I sat behind the glass window on the hard, plastic seat and tried to figure out if it was possibly someone other than my mom who sat across from me. I'd seen her in a down mood before, but not like this. What was wrong with her?

"I got here as soon as I could, Mom. It's been tough to get a ride here. But my friend, Ginny, was able to bring me today."

Mom glared, kept her arms crossed. "Well, what a rough time you've had. So sorry to hear that your free life outside of jail is so difficult. Meanwhile, here I am, rotting alone in this miserable hell hole."

Was she for real? "I've been missing you every day, but maybe I shouldn't be. Have you thought about what it's like for me with a mom in jail?"

I cringed at the last thing I said. Her eyes widened, she uncrossed her arms, leaned into the window, her face centimeters from the glass. Her voice sounded a little like one of those evil witches in the Disney movies we used to watch. "How dare you talk to me that way. You have no idea what I'm going through."

I wanted to reach through the glass and shake her. I was so angry, but I didn't have time to argue and fall into her pity party.

"So, what's up with Richard?" I asked, shutting down my desire to cry. I hated having to play tough, not letting her know how sad I was. I hated that I couldn't be myself around her anymore.

Her anger turned to phony surprise. "What do you mean what's up with Richard? I wouldn't really know. I broke up the engagement yesterday. We aren't speaking anymore."

What? I didn't think something good could happen from going to jail, but maybe their break up was it. But on a bad note, that was probably why Richard took Jared. There was no reason to stay around anymore. He was fleeing with my very best friend.

"Mom, Richard just took Jared. They're going to our house.

Do you know what's going on? Is Jared in danger? Should I go to the police?" Mom's gaze turned downward. She didn't look me in the eye. She knew something.

"I understand your concern for Jared," she said at last, "but his father won't hurt him, and the police won't do anything unless Jared is in actual danger. He's not being kidnapped. He's with his own father. You should be grateful he didn't take you as well. Stay away from him."

Did she really think I should feel grateful? How was that possible? "Well, I can't stay away. Jared asked me to meet him at the house, which means he must need my help. I can't ignore that."

"Emily, do not meet him, you hear me? Jared will be okay."

"If he's going to be okay, why is it unsafe for me to meet him? I can't just not show up. Jared means everything to me."

"Why is Jared so important to you?" She looked me straight in the eyes, that look she always gave when she meant business and wanted me to know it. For the first time ever, I didn't care.

"Seriously? Why is Jared so important to me? Well, let's think about it, Mom. My dad took off before I ever got to know him, my mom is in jail, and my grandmother is a bit crazy. So Jared is it, Mom, get it?" I still wanted to find out why she had lied to me about my dad trying to get in touch with me, but I didn't bring it up. I was more worried about Jared, and based on her mood, I figured I wouldn't get a good response.

She kept her death stare on me. "Yes, Emily. I get it, but I can't tell you anything. That won't help you. Staying away will."

"Fine, don't tell me, but tell the police whatever it is you know. Let them catch Richard. Then he can be in jail where he belongs and maybe you can get out. He's the reason you sold those drugs, Mom. You would have never done that if he didn't make you do it. He turned you into this person I don't know anymore."

She looked pained after I said that. She closed her eyes,

took a deep breath. "Emily, this isn't something you can solve. Richard leaving is probably the best solution we'll ever get. Let him go."

"Okay, fine. I'll stop asking you for help. Obviously that's not your job anymore, to help me, so I'll figure it out myself." I stood up, the metal chair scraping across the concrete floors. I placed my hand on the glass, the same way I had during my last visit. "I love you, Mom," I said, tears wetting my hot cheeks. "I'm going to our home to see Jared, and if he's in danger, I'll help him."

I turned to walk away. I could hear her screaming through the glass, "Emily, please! Let it go! Come back and listen to me! Please!" I heard fists pounding the glass. I glanced back for a second and wished I hadn't. The guards pulled her away as she kicked and swung and screamed. I felt like I'd lost my mom forever.

# –21–

Once I was outside, I couldn't walk. My wimpy tears turned to gut wrenching sobs. I held my stomach, inched my way to a brick planter, so out of place with its bright tulips. Why did anyone bother to plant anything beautiful there? Why would they even try to make jail look cheery? Dirt, dust, hot cement—those things belonged in such a miserable place.

I felt a hand on my shoulder. "Hey, my friend." Ginny pulled me into a hug and let me cry, no questions asked, no telling me things would be okay. That's how I knew she understood me. She never tried to sugarcoat things that she knew simply sucked. "I take it things didn't go so well in there," she said.

"Not at all," I said between heaving breaths, trying to calm down. "I got nothing out of her, Ginny. She won't tell me anything about Richard except that he's dangerous and I should stay away. She says Jared will be fine, but how is that possible if Richard is dangerous? I'm not afraid of that man. I'm more afraid to do nothing. I'm terrified I'll never see Jared again."

"Okay, then let's go get him."

I loved this girl. She was with me, one hundred percent. She said the things I thought but somehow couldn't say out loud. "You're not afraid of anything, are you?" I asked.

She looked up, tapped her finger on her chin, "Hmmm, let

me think. Nope, nothing. So, to your old place?"

"I guess so. I wish I was heading home for a better reason, but I guess this is it."

I'd thought about home every day since I'd left it a week ago, but now that I was about to visit, I had mixed feelings. Home used to be the place where there was some security, some happiness. But it wasn't at all like that when I left, and the thought of facing Richard didn't feel good either. No matter how much I said I wasn't afraid of him, deep down I knew my mom was right. He was capable of a lot of bad stuff.

"Okay, you got it. Just tell me how to get there," Ginny said.

Off we went again, back to the wildest ride on earth, but this time, I didn't really care. Getting there was all that mattered.

It was a little before six when we reached the familiar neighborhood streets of Ridgeway. We passed the twenty-something-year-old who lived around the corner, out on her evening run. I spotted the young nurse who worked at the hospital and walked home every night in her white uniform. Ginny nearly ran into two boys on their skateboards who weaved back and forth in the bike lane, then jumped onto the sidewalk. The sky was tinted orange and purple above the hillside of homes ahead. We drove into those hills, along the street I trudged up when I had to walk home from school.

"Turn at the next street," I told Ginny. "My house is the third one on the right, but don't stop. I want to make sure no one is outside who might see me, and I want to see if we see Jared's truck."

No lights were on in Mr. Cardeen's house, so he probably wasn't home yet, and the house on the other side still had a realtor sign on the lawn. It had been up for sale months before Mom's arrest when the owners, the Thompsons, moved back to Chicago to be closer to their kids and grandchildren. They seemed like the best parents, hosting big family gatherings when their grown boys' families came home to visit. I could hear their laughter through my window, see the brothers throwing a football in the yard with their kids. I could always smell something cooking, sausage and coffee in the morning, cookies in the afternoons, something warm and spicy in the evening. When Mom was gone a lot, I wished I could knock on the Thompsons' door and invite myself in for a meal, or a snack, even a cup of water while I sat back and pretended I was part of them.

"Park in front of this house with the For Sale sign," I told Ginny as I pointed to the Thompsons' house. "It'll look like someone's here to look at the house. I don't see Jared's truck, so unless they parked somewhere else, they must not be here yet. I guess we should go hide in the back until they arrive."

Ginny pulled up along the curb. "Nice place," Ginny said, looking instead at my house. The lawn was overgrown with long grass and dandelions. The geraniums Mom so carefully tended were dead. A flattened McDonald's cup and a yellow, weathered newspaper decorated our lawn, reminding me of what our family had become, trash.

"It used to look a lot better," I said.

I could hear kids playing in the yard across the street. I saw a woman walk her Corgi around the corner. Life appeared normal as I watched it from the car. I wished that were the case.

"Okay, well, I'll follow you." Ginny pulled the keys from the ignition and plopped them in her yellow pleather purse.

I pushed open the car door and stepped out. I peered to my left, no one there, to my right, all clear, behind me, good. I approached the side gate, reached my hand over the top to unlatch the hook, prepared to push all my weight into it to force it open. But the gate wasn't latched, and it opened easily.

"Weird," I said to Ginny. "All these years I've had to wrestle with this gate, and now, when the house has supposedly been secured by police, it just glides open."

I walked through the side yard, Ginny close behind. I heard someone talking. "Wait, there's someone here," I whispered to Ginny. We stepped carefully, but a stick under my foot cracked and the talking stopped. I stood frozen. Maybe they'd think it was a rabbit or a squirrel. Maybe they'd go back to their conversation, whoever it was. I began to creep along the edge of the wall, watching my feet this time so as not to step on anything. I peeked around the corner.

Richard stood there. He held a gun in his hand, and it was aimed right at me.

# –22–

I've watched tons of television shows where someone is behind the barrel of a gun. The person facing this threat runs at the guy holding the gun as if that would stop the bullet. Or, they magically pull a gun out of their own pocket and shoot first, or someone comes from nowhere and saves the person about to be shot. None of these scenarios were happening for me.

"Dad, put the gun down. It's Emily." Jared spoke from behind Richard. I was pretty sure Richard had registered who I was by now, but he still wasn't lowering the gun. The only thing that distracted my sight from his weapon was Richard's bright neon green gloves with a blue stripe across the fingertips.

"Yeah, I see who it is, Jared, and I'll bet she's got someone with her too. Right, Emily?"

I had no idea how to answer that or why it mattered.

"Dad, put the gun down. She's harmless and you know it."

Richard clearly didn't think so. I saw his thumb press down on the hammer of the gun, heard the clicking sound guns make before they fire. He stepped closer. "Who you got there with ya, Em? Someone who might be lookin' for me? Someone who thinks I owe him money?"

I wanted to back away, but I couldn't get my legs to budge.

I wanted to speak, but my mouth was parched, numb, incapable of a scream. I saw Ginny, no longer behind me, but in front of me. What was she doing? *Move, Ginny! Move!* I screamed in my head.

I wanted to push her away, but my arms were as worthless and stiff as the rest of me. Jared moved instead. He grabbed Richard, bumping his arm, setting off that sound, the explosion that makes people panic and run, the blast that pierced my ears, followed by the heavy thump of Ginny's body hitting the ground. Beneath her head, that head so full of wit and courage and smarts, ran a trail of blood.

Screams belted out of me, unstoppable, uncontrollable from deep within. I heard Jared, shouting at Richard, then the thump, thump, thump of Richard's footsteps, running toward me, then past me, past Ginny, as if she were nothing, as if all that blood didn't matter. Jared sprinted past next, chasing Richard. "Call 911, Em! Hurry! Call now!" He pulled his phone from the front pocket of his jeans and tossed it to me.

"Right, 911," I said aloud to no one. My head spun as blood pooled beneath Ginny's head. The gun lay on the ground beside her. My hand shook uncontrollably, but I managed to touch it and slide it out of the way.

*Don't pass out, Em. Don't pass out.* I leaned next to Ginny's mouth. I could feel her breath. "Ginny? Can you hear me?" Nothing.

I put my head to her chest, touched her wrist, felt for a pulse. Still beating. My hands shook uncontrollably as I clumsily dialed 911, my fingers wobbling around over the numbers, my eyes blurry with tears. Finally, someone spoke on the other end and I found my voice.

"My friend has been shot. Please help me!"

I gave the operator my address and she told me to stay on the line until paramedics arrived. She talked me through how to check her pulse and breathing, which I had already done, but

I did again anyway. I couldn't think, like I was being controlled by someone else, like this was all just a bad dream and I would wake up soon.

What I wanted was for the lady on the phone to tell me how to get Ginny up, to open her eyes and say, "Hey, Em, what's up? Let's go get that jerk who just shot me." That was the Ginny I knew, never held back by any challenge that came her way. But that wasn't happening now. A gunshot to the head was one thing Ginny couldn't laugh off.

I heard sirens approaching, "They're here," I said to the 911 operator. I hung up the phone and begged, "Please, help her," which was a plea to the ambulance screeching to a stop, but even more, it was my first real prayer to God.

# -23-

The back gate swung open as three police officers ran through. They each held their guns out in front of them, looked from side to side as they stepped cautiously toward Ginny and me. The older and larger of them shouted, "Where's the shooter?"

"He's gone! He ran out the gate! My friend chased after him. Can someone please go help him? And can someone please help my friend?" I shouted through my sobs. I felt dizzy, like I might pass out.

"James, Colton, go! Now!" He nodded his head in the direction of the gate, but kept his gun ready in front of him. He continued to look around and headed toward me as several more armed police entered the yard and scattered in different directions, apparently looking to see if anyone else was still there.

Finally, two paramedics entered. They set down their stretcher, a big red medical bag, and stood on each side of Ginny.

"We're going to need some room here, Miss. Are you okay?" One of them said. He pushed his hand through short, buzz cut hair, stared down at Ginny and the blood beneath her as he pulled gloves onto his hands.

"Yeah, I'm okay." I got up as quickly as I could, hoping I wouldn't feel any dizzier and fall back down.

"What's her name?" Buzz-cut-paramedic asked as he kneeled beside Ginny and rested his fingers along her neck to check her pulse.

"Ginny," I replied. I felt so helpless as he called her name, asked if she could hear him, told the other paramedic holding Ginny's head between his hands that she had a pulse, shallow breathing, pale skin color.

"Excuse me, Miss?" The police officer I first spoke to stood tall next to me. His voice was deep and commanding, his presence huge, but he had a round face and kind brown eyes that made me feel safe. "I'm Sergeant Artis. I'm going to need you to tell me your name and what you saw happen here. How about if we step away and sit down? You don't look so good."

He gently grasped my arm and led me to a chair at the patio table where I used to sit and have relaxing meals with Mom. How had this home become a place of such trauma?

I told Sergeant Artis my name, described what had happened the best I could without throwing up while he took detailed notes of everything I said. I stopped talking when I saw the paramedics carrying Ginny on the stretcher. "Is she okay?" I yelled.

"We're doing all we can. We're on our way to Mercy Hospital.

I felt like I needed to run toward Ginny as the paramedics continued to walk away, but my body wouldn't move. I forced myself to stand. "Wait! Can I go? I can't leave her. I need to be with her."

Before they responded, Sergeant Artis stood and put his hands on my shoulders, squared me toward him, and looked at me with sympathetic eyes. "Hey, I'll take you. Trust me. That will be better than riding on the ambulance. Let them do what they need to do to help your friend."

It was as if part of me was ripped away as Ginny rode off without me. Before today I thought a ride in an ambulance might be a thrill, speeding through the streets while everyone moved out of the way. But there was nothing fun about an ambulance when your friend was possibly dying in one.

I had to finish giving my official statement of what happened before we left for the hospital. I was actually relieved to be with Sergeant Artis once inside his car. It felt good to sit down without the sight of blood, without seeing Ginny look like she was dead. While we sped away, I closed my eyes and imagined the paramedics bringing her back to life in the ambulance. I took deep breaths to keep from passing out.

I heard Sergeant Artis's voice, smooth and calming, "Hang in there, Emily. You're gonna get through this." I wished I believed that.

Sergeant Artis pulled up to the curb, and we got out to enter the Emergency Room. The air outside was cool, quiet, a calm breeze blowing. But once the automatic doors opened, we entered a storm. A baby cried in his mother's arms, an elderly man pushed his wife in a wheelchair, a young man held an icepack to a gash on his forehead, a woman held her side with one hand and rocked back and forth as if to distract from the pain she obviously felt. It was shocking to see that many people all needing help at the same time. I refocused my attention on Sergeant Artis. He was the calm in this chaos.

He walked with confidence to a young nurse at the check in desk. "We're here for Ginny Bartle. The paramedics brought her in," he said.

"No problem, one moment." She picked up the phone on the desk next to her and asked whoever answered for an update on Ginny. It seemed like forever while she listened to the response. She tapped her pen on the desk, smoothed back a wispy blonde hair that escaped her pony tail. I tried to read her face for an answer, but she managed to maintain the same calm expression as she nodded her head to whoever spoke on the other end.

Finally she hung up and said, "The ER nurse said she was brought into surgery. You'll need to check in at the main lobby and let them direct you to the operating room waiting area. The staff there will be able to keep you informed." She smiled and turned her attention to a frazzled mom and her coughing, crying baby behind us.

"Thank you," Sergeant Artis said as he placed his hand on my shoulder, directing me to turn back toward the emergency room doors. I robotically followed his lead as we walked out of the noise, to the brisk night air outside, into the main doors of the hospital.

After we checked in, we went to the waiting area, where the temperature was still as freezing as the emergency room, but at least the chairs were cushioned and there was artwork on the walls. Tables between the chairs were covered with magazines, tissue boxes, and hospital brochures. A lady with a preschool aged child asleep on her lap slumped in one chair. She held a tissue to her eyes as she spoke through tears to the bearded man next to her. An older lady sat several seats over, reading a book, kind of looking like she'd done this before.

Sergeant Artis directed me to have a seat while he brought me a cup of coffee that I somehow said yes to when he offered. I didn't even like coffee, but I took it in my hands and soaked in its warmth. It reminded me of Mom. She would have had a cup in this situation. She loved coffee. It was the closest I could get to her comforting arms.

While I sipped, Sergeant Artis told me to sit tight while he made a phone call. I heard him talking to someone about getting the phone number and address of the Bartles as he stepped away. The thought of Ginny's parents hearing this news was a punch to my gut. They would never forgive me.

I drank the coffee methodically, one slow and bitter sip after another, only because it sort of distracted me from what was happening. I stared at the dark liquid, took a sip, swirled it around, took another sip, kept doing this until it was gone. When Sergeant Artis returned, I wasn't sure if my heart was racing from the caffeine or what he said next.

"We've called Ginny's parents. They're on the way. Your grandmother didn't answer, but we'll try again." He stood tall in front of me, making me feel safe for the moment. I was glad he was handling everything, but I wished I hadn't given him Grandma's number, made up a phony one instead. She would be so disappointed that I lied to her about what I was doing.

"You don't have to call her. I can do that." I didn't know if I would, but I hoped that would keep him from calling. I needed to figure out how to explain all this to her. I didn't want the police to be the ones to do that.

"Well, as a minor involved in a crime scene, I have to contact your guardian and make sure you return home safely, but of course you can call her too."

So much for that plan of keeping the police out of it, and the thought of Ginny's parents knowing wasn't any better. I hated to think of their reaction when the police called. Surely they panicked. And what about Mrs. Bartle's car? Did she rush to the parking lot only to think that her car was stolen? I suddenly felt like a criminal myself. Ginny drove to help me, to make sure I was okay. I should never have let her. I should have never gone to my house. I should have listened to my mom. It might as well have been me who put that bullet in Ginny's head.

# –24–

Ginny's parents arrived in a flurry of panic. I sat frozen in the waiting room chair. I wanted to crawl under it, melt away slowly and quietly. But they dashed past without noticing me, straight to the nurse's station.

"Where's my daughter?" Mrs. Bartle said frantically. "I'm her mother."

Mr. Bartle remained quiet with his hand on his wife's back, but his stance was everything but quiet. He loomed large over Mrs. Bartle, leaning in to listen to one of the nurse's answer, his free hand clenched tight at his side.

The nurse rose from her desk and said, "If you hold on one moment, I'll go get an update on your daughter."

"No, I'll go with you. I need to see her. I'm a nurse. I can help." Mrs. Bartle raised her voice, sounded desperate.

"Ma'am, we can't let you come while she's in surgery. I'll get a status on how things are going and how long it will be before you can see her."

Mrs. Bartle looked up at Mr. Bartle, a pleading look for help. I knew she was aware of hospital procedure, but clearly she was in mom mode.

"We understand," he said in his firm, deep tone. "But be quick. We shouldn't have to wait long, and I want the name of the doctor caring for her."

"Yes, sir," the nurse responded, "I'll be back as soon as I have the update." She darted away, and Mrs. Bartle buried her head into Mr. Bartle's chest, sobbing.

I wanted to jump up and run away even though I knew I should greet them. But my feet felt heavy, stuck, like my life. I watched Mrs. Bartle pull back from Mr. Bartle as Sergeant Artis approached them and began to speak. A few seconds later, Mrs. Bartle rubbed a tissue to her eyes, turned in my direction, and locked eyes with me.

The death glare I expected, the one that showed blame, disgust hate, did not appear. Instead, I saw eyes that showed sympathy and love, the kind I felt certain only a mom knew how to give. I missed those kind of mom eyes.

"Oh, Emily," she cried. She ran toward me, her arms stretched wide in front of her, and as soon as she reached me, she pulled me into a huge embrace. Once in it, I realized how much I needed it. I felt a mountain of both sadness and relief well up in me, and I let it all out, crying like I never had before.

"Emily, I'm so glad you were with her when this happened. Thank you for taking care of her, for getting help so quickly."

I couldn't get myself to say you're welcome. She didn't know the whole story. She probably thought this was some random act of violence, not a gunshot from my mom's former fiancé.

I stayed in her hug, but pulled my head away enough to say, "Mrs. Bartle, I'm so sorry, so, so sorry."

She pulled herself away from me, held my face between her hands. "Oh, Emily, it's not your fault. It's an absolute horrible thing, done by an absolutely horrible person, but it's not your fault."

I wanted to believe her, to think I had nothing to do with this, but I was scared to no end to tell her who shot Ginny. Mr. Bartle kept rubbing a trembling hand along Mrs. Bartle's back.

He tapped his foot and turned his head away every few seconds toward the door the nurse had entered when she went to check on Ginny. Finally, the nurse came through those doors.

"Mr. and Mrs. Bartle, I have some news on your daughter," the nurse said when she reached us.

Mr. and Mrs. Bartle both looked pale, frozen.

"The doctor was able to remove the bullet."

"Oh, thank God," Mrs. Bartle exhaled and squeezed my hand.

"Oh, yes, thank you," Mr. Bartle said, like he'd been holding his breath all this time.

The nurse continued, "The doctor can give you more definitive results once Ginny is out of surgery. He'll come speak with you while she's in recovery, probably about thirty more minutes."

"Does this mean she'll be okay?" Mrs. Bartle asked. "Will there be any permanent brain damage?"

Mrs. Bartle was so used to being on the opposite end of all this. She knew how many horrible things could be wrong. Her head was probably like the internet, searching and finding all the possible outcomes.

"I'm sorry, Mrs. Bartle, I don't have details other than the bullet was safely removed. The doctor will answer any other questions. Can I get you anything while you wait? Some water? Coffee?" The nurse seemed desperate to distract Mrs. Bartle. I got the feeling she knew more than she was saying.

Mrs. Bartle turned down the coffee, which was a sure sign of her worry. Ginny once told me her mom drank coffee like it was water, like it was the source of all the body's needed hydration. She said she even drank it when working out, which seemed like a really bad idea.

Once the nurse left, I knew I was the only one who could answer the Bartles' questions and I knew what the first question would be.

It was Mr. Bartle who asked it. "What exactly happened, Emily?"

Yep, that was the question I knew was coming my way. The one that once answered would turn the Bartles from loving me to hating me, deservedly. I wished I could lie or make the story better in some way, but I couldn't come up with anything other than the truth.

"I'm so sorry, Mrs. Bartle." I looked into her eyes, only for a second, and knew I couldn't get through this if I didn't glance away. I stared at the hospital floor, white-tiled with gray speckles, as cheerless and drab as I felt.

"It's all my fault. She shouldn't have come, and I should have listened to my mom."

"Emily, nothing is your fault unless you were the one shooting the gun," Mrs. Bartle replied, rubbing my shoulder with her hand.

"Jared's dad shot her, Mrs. Bartle. I'm so sorry. Ginny was trying to help me, and she got hurt."

"Jared's dad?" Mrs. Bartle asked, casting a glance at her husband. "I didn't think he was around since you and Jared moved in with your grandma. I thought he was in jail."

"I wish, especially now." I thought of Jared once again and wondered where he was, if he was okay, if the police had found him, found Richard. Then I filled Ginny's parents in on the entire story, how Ginny took her mother's car, how we went to visit my mom first. I told her everything.

Mrs. Bartle pulled away from me. I knew that was coming. I would pull away from me too, if I could.

"Honey, look at me. In the eyes, not down at that floor, but right here." She leaned her head low so I couldn't avoid her face, and pointed to her eyes. It was the first time in a long time that I had actually made eye contact with someone. Her eyes were hazel, more green than brown, eyeliner smudged below her lower lid, her eyelashes clumped together from the combination of thick mascara and wet tears.

"Okay, now that I have your attention, listen up," she continued. "You are not responsible for what Jared's father did. Obviously he is a depraved, sick man, but you're not the reason Ginny is lying in that hospital bed, and I meant it when I said thank God you were with her. I know you haven't known her long, but she has become a new person since she met you." Mrs. Bartle looked away for a moment. She continued, speaking through her tears. "You are the first girl to befriend her in a very long time. She's always been criticized for her size. Since sixth grade, she's been taunted as Giant Ginny, the girl no one wanted as a friend. I'm angry at *him*, not you. You have not been treated right by people in our town either, Emily. You deserve better."

The same way Ginny had been tagged Giant Ginny, I was branded as the druggie's daughter. Most parents probably wanted their children to steer clear of me. Mr. and Mrs. Bartle didn't. Mrs. Bartle wrapped her arms around me, pulled me in. She was the first parent since Mom had left who wanted to hold me close.

# –25–

I clung to Mrs. Bartle like I used to hang on to Mom after a bad dream.

"Emily!"

I looked up and saw Jared pacing toward us. He limped, his pants torn at the knee, muddy and stained with dry blood. Mrs. Bartle loosened her hold as I moved toward him.

"Jared," I hugged him tight as tears erupted. "I thought I was going to lose you, Jared. I'm so glad you're here. Are you okay? You're limping. And what happened to Richard?"

"Well, lucky for us, I'm faster than him. I caught up to him about ten houses down from yours, knocked him to the ground, and held him there. He tried to break away, but also lucky for us, he's not stronger than me anymore. The police got there while he was yelling at me to let go, saying he'd turn himself in."

"Of course he said that, always lying to get his way. How could he think you'd believe that?"

While I knew Jared was glad his dad was caught, he looked so, so sad. "I don't understand anything my dad says or does. I can't believe we're even related. But the weird thing is, as much as I hate him, I still love him. Does that make any sense?

I knew exactly what he meant, loving and hating at the same

time. "Yes, absolutely. It makes a lot of sense, Jared."

He continued, "The worst part was hearing him cry. I thought I was hurting his arm or something, but then he said, 'I love you, Jared. I'm so sorry. I love you.' That nearly broke me. I can't remember him saying that to me, ever. Why did he have to say it now? I wanted to let go of him and hug him, but I couldn't. I couldn't trust that he meant it when he said he loved me."

I grabbed Jared's hands as tears rolled down his cheeks. He was always so solid, but this had broken him, and I couldn't stand it. I pulled him into a hug and prayed. *God, please help him. I don't know how. Please, please help Jared.*

When I finally pulled away, I looked up at him and said, "We're going to get through this, Jared, okay? Our parents might suck right now, but we've got each other. That's what keeps getting me through everything."

Jared cracked a slight smile. "Yeah, me too, Em. I couldn't do this without you."

"So, what was he getting from the house anyway? Did you ever find out?"

Jared shook his head, a look of disgust on his face. "Yeah, he started digging up the backyard with a shovel, kept going until he was like four feet down, and uncovered this big metal box. He laughed and acted all excited, opened it, and inside were a bunch of guns. That was right before you and Ginny came. When he heard you, he pulled out a gun and headed towards you. You know what happened after that."

Jared stopped and took a deep breath, looked at me with eyes filled with tears and the nightmare of what we both had seen. "He should have never been allowed to get a gun, Emily. This never would have happened if he didn't have a stupid gun."

Tears rolled down his cheeks as he let this out. I grabbed his hands and held them tight. I knew how horrible he felt, and I hated to see him that way. I tried to think of something to say to make him feel better, but I knew there weren't any words that would help.

The sight of a doctor coming our way caught my attention. He was tall, dark hair with a few gray strands, and had that straight face doctors have where you can't tell if they're about to give good news or bad. If I were a doctor who pulled a bullet from someone's skull and everything was fine, I'd skip down the hospital hall, hug my patient's loved ones and shout, "Yes! We did it! All is well!" But I've never seen a doctor do that.

"Mr. and Mrs. Bartle?" he asked.

"Yes," Mrs. Bartle said. Her hand gripped her husband's. I folded my arms tight in front of me, trying to warm up from the chilly hospital air.

"I'm Dr. Spalding, the chief neurosurgeon here." He held a clipboard in his left arm, glanced at it quickly and then looked back to the Bartles. "We were successful at removing the bullet from your daughter's left temporal lobe. She is stable and in ICU."

"Thank you so much, Dr. Spalding. We're so grateful. But how is she?" Mrs. Bartle spoke through tears in a tone that begged for the truth. She obviously knew that removing the bullet didn't mean Ginny was okay.

He still didn't look like someone delivering happy news. He looked at Mrs. Bartle with the same serious expression, brows furrowed, no smile. "We're going to keep her in ICU for a while. Direct family will be allowed to visit her, and then others can see her when she moves to another room." He paused for a second.

Here it came, the bad side of the news. "It's important to understand that recovery from this type of injury varies from patient to patient. Ginny incurred trauma to the left hemisphere of her brain, which is mainly responsible for functions such as vision, language, and the ability to move the right side of the body. Patients recovering from this type of injury mostly have difficulty reading, speaking, understanding speech. Fortunately, we were able to treat Ginny shortly after her injury, so there was less time for swelling. Also, the way the bullet penetrated miraculously left the brain structures intact."

Mr. and Mrs. Bartle stood frozen. It was like they wanted to say something, but couldn't, like they maybe heard what he said, but hadn't processed it. Dr. Spalding must have noticed.

"Patients can be near normal within four to six months, but every patient is unique. I will be seeing Ginny regularly and she will need therapy, so I will give you the name of our rehab therapists as well." He paused and took a deep breath. "My hope is that she will recover well, but you need to be prepared for the possibility that she may not. Permanent damage is possible. We will do everything we can for her."

Mrs. Bartle finally unfroze, but there was still no color in her face. "Oh my God, no, she doesn't deserve this. Speaking is her thing. My funny, witty daughter has to be able to talk. I think I can handle anything but that."

Dr. Spalding put his hand on Mrs. Bartle's shoulder. "I'm so sorry. I know it's frightening and unnerving that we can't give you definite answers."

Permanent damage. Those words sunk into my gut. Permanent damage. I couldn't picture Ginny without speech, without sarcastic comments flying off her tongue, without her boldly honest advice. That's what made Ginny so real, so genuine, so alive. I was afraid of what I thought when I first heard that gunshot in the backyard hours ago; I was terrified I had lost the new friend whose confidence and words and laughter had been helping me to find life.

# —26—

No matter how hard and uncomfortable the hospital waiting room chairs were, no matter how much I wished to be in a soft bed under a comfy blanket, I didn't want to leave that hospital. I wanted to wait until Ginny got up, walked down the hall, into the waiting room and said, "What is all the fuss about? I'm fine. Let's go." But Jared, as usual, snapped me back to reality.

"We should probably get home. I know you want to be here when Ginny wakes up, but that's not going to happen tonight, and we're not allowed in to see her yet anyway. While you were sleeping, Sergeant Artis spoke to me. He said he talked to your grandma, told her what had happened, and that we should be on our way back tonight."

I pictured the disappointment etched on Grandma's face when I was suspended from school two days ago. That was horrible to see, but at least I wasn't guilty then. This time I was. I had lied to her. I had gone to see my mom when she had told me to wait. I let Ginny drive without a license and then somehow managed to put her in front of a gun. I knew Grandma's expression would show more than disappointment after all this.

"I am so afraid to face her. She must be so sad and sorry that she took me in."

"She is not going to be sorry she took you in. She's definitely going to be upset that you lied to her, but not sorry she has you. I get the feeling she really cares about us, and she doesn't seem to get mad easily."

As much as I wanted to believe him, I didn't. We were silent for most of the drive back to Grandma's. I kept replaying the gunshot, Ginny's body on the ground, a hospital bed with Ginny lying in it, unable to talk. I needed to sleep, but I felt better awake, where I could at least look out the window and see things other than those images.

Staring at the road made me think about the poem by Robert Frost, "The Road Not Taken." We read it in my eighth grade English class. It had reminded me that the right path wasn't always the popular one, or the one that always turned out how we thought it should. Every time I had traveled along this stretch of highway toward Grandma's, I wished I didn't have to be on it. It seemed like the wrong way. It had led me away from my mom, my friends, my home. But this time I actually felt like I was on the way toward home. I felt relieved, like I was heading toward something much better than what I was leaving behind.

But before I could enjoy complete relief, the ring of Jared's phone reminded me of what I still had to face. It was Grandma.

"Oh no, what do we do?" I asked while holding the phone so Jared could see who it was.

Jared didn't look panicked like me. "She's probably wondering where we are and wants to know we're okay. I think you need to pick it up."

"But what do I say? I don't want to explain everything on the phone." His ringtone seemed louder than normal, like it was screaming at me.

"Tell her we're okay, we'll be home in an hour, and we'll explain when we get there. Then hang up before she can ask any questions."

That sounded good, but I wasn't sure I could be that short with her. She deserved more. I pushed the button to answer, held the phone to my ear, took a deep breath, and then froze.

"Emily? Emily dear, are you there?" Grandma had a panic in her voice I'd never heard before.

I let out all my breath and forced out words I wished had the power to tear down my mountain of mistakes.

"I'm so sorry, Grandma. I shouldn't have lied to you. I should have listened to you and waited to go see Mom. But instead, Ginny took me, and then we went to my house after, and that's when . . . that's when . . ."

All this spilled out of me, but I couldn't finish. I couldn't retell what happened at my house. I saw Ginny again, on the ground, and it was like I was there again. My hands shook. I couldn't breathe.

"Emily? Emily, it's okay." I heard Jared say, but it was like he was miles away. I closed my eyes tight, trying to squeeze Ginny's image out of my head, trying to quiet the gun sound meshed with the doctor's words. Permanent. Damage. Permanent. Damage.

"Emily," I felt Jared's hand on my shoulder and looked up to see we weren't moving. We were on the side of the road. "Are you okay?" Jared asked. "Are you with me?"

"Emily? Emily! Are you there? Are you okay?" I heard Grandma's voice coming from my phone.

"I'm here, Grandma. I'm okay," I said, even though I didn't feel okay at all. I tried to slow my breath. "I'm here. I'm okay," I repeated. Something about saying it again calmed me. I heard it again in my head. *I'm here, and I'm okay.*

Those simple words somehow felt so powerful. Being alive, being okay. The two things I'd never thought too much about were suddenly so appreciated. Jared pulled back onto the highway, and this time when I closed my eyes, I felt my lungs fill with air, long and slow, into sleep.

# –27–

Jared parked in front of the house, turned the engine off. We sat there for several minutes in the dark silence.

"It's a little sad that she's not greeting us outside like she normally does." The porch light glowed on her dusty yard and cast a shadow of her tree's leaves dancing in the wind. I remembered the dull little pebble she had found in that dirt and placed in my hands. I stared at my palms, now empty, and felt a pit in my stomach.

"Hey, it's late. She's probably asleep, and she didn't sound mad at you on the phone. She sounded worried about us. She's going to be glad we're finally here, safe."

"Yeah, okay. I hope you're right." I felt like I did before the start of a race, filled with dread and wonder over what might happen in the next several minutes. *You got this*, were the words I would repeat in my mind then, so I tried that now.

I sat there, trying to move, and somehow I remembered one night when I came home late from Brit's house. The only reason I was late was because Brit and I got caught up in watching stupid movies, then even dumber videos on our phones, and then talking about boys we liked, girls who annoyed us, and who should go out with who if we were in charge of the world. But Mom had heard about some party down the street when one of the moms from school brought it up at the grocery store.

"So, you went to the party, didn't you?" she asked the second I came in the door. She was sitting on the couch with all the lights out but one, like she'd been waiting there all night.

"Mom, why would we go to a party where we weren't even invited?" I said, feeling annoyed that I would need to explain this to her.

"Oh, like that's going to convince me. You don't need an invite to get into that kind of party. You just need to show up in some cute little outfit and you'll get in."

That comment made me mad. Did she really think that's something I'd do? Did she see what I was currently wearing? Pajama bottoms and a track sweatshirt. Did she remember that I had practice the next morning at seven and had to run however many crazy miles our coach felt like assigning? Neither of those should hint that I wanted to party.

"Mom, we were at Brit's house. Her mom bought ingredients to make cookies for the track bake sale, and then we watched movies and talked. We didn't want to go to the party. I can't believe I have to say this, but why don't you call her mom if you don't trust me? Clearly I've done something in between earning good grades and running tons of miles every day to make you suspicious of me."

I knew my sarcasm was disrespectful, but I didn't care. She had been acting different, getting angry easier, staying home from work because she couldn't wake up. She told me she was disgusted with me, told me to go upstairs, grounded me. Even though I'd done nothing wrong, I was so sad she was displeased with me, and so clueless about what was wrong with her.

I snapped back to my current reality when I walked into Grandma's house. She sat at the table with a cup of tea and a box of tissue. When she looked up, I could tell she'd been crying.

"Hi Grandma," I said, feeling so absolutely horrible.

"Oh, Emily, Jared, I'm so glad to see you." She stood up and rushed toward me, her arms wide. She pulled me close into a tight hug. Then she stared up at me and touched my face gently before hugging Jared.

"I know you two don't normally drink tea, but would you like some tonight? It's really quite calming. I think it might be good for you."

I wasn't going to turn her down. I figured she needed us to drink some tea more than we needed it. "Sure, that would be nice."

Her face lit up. Who'd have thought saying yes to tea could make someone that much happier. "Well, that's wonderful. Come and have a seat."

As she grabbed two cups, I noticed her hands shaking. She began pouring the tea and missed my cup, then bumped it over as she tried to reposition the teapot. "Oh heavens, I'm sorry," she said. She grabbed the cup quickly, set the teapot back on the table, but accidentally set it partially on the dish of leaves she must have collected that day, and the tea pot fell sideways. "Oh my goodness, what is wrong with me?" She said with her hands still shaking, but now hovering over the spilled tea, afraid to touch anything.

"Hey, it's okay. We got this." Jared put his arm around her as I picked up the teapot and soaked up the tea with napkins.

Grandma placed one hand on Jared's as it rested on her shoulder. She brushed her other hand across her cheeks as tears rolled down them.

"Grandma, I'm so sorry." I knew I'd already said this on the phone, but I had to say it again. I didn't know what else to do. "I hope you don't regret that we came to live with you. I hope you don't send us somewhere else."

Breaking down in tears, I looked at Jared. He kept rubbing Grandma's shoulder as she squeezed his hand tight in hers. Then she sat down, reached across the table and grabbed my hand.

"Oh, Emily. I am not going to send you anywhere. You are my granddaughter, and Jared, you're like a grandson to me, even if we're not flesh and blood. I could never think of not having you in my life now that you've entered it. That's why I was so upset, thinking something horrible had happened to you. But now, I'm so thankful you're okay."

Jared was right. She really did love us, so much that she didn't seem to have any anger at what I'd done. I didn't know why I hadn't noticed that sooner, or realized how much I loved her. Maybe that was what Grandma meant about God making all things good. Somehow in all the bad stuff, I felt something undeniably wonderful.

# –28–

The next couple weeks were slow, no Ginny, school where everyone asked way too many questions and looked at me either as they did before, but with even more disgust, or with extreme pity, like I was some sick animal who couldn't be helped.

I tried to focus on something other than Ginny, but it was rough. One Friday evening, I sat at the kitchen table trying to catch up on homework. Jared had told me the day before that he renewed my phone service with some of his savings money. When I told him he shouldn't have done that, he told me he was doing it for himself because he wanted to be able to reach me in an emergency. After all we had been through, it was difficult to argue his point. So, now with a working phone, no school the next day, and my mind consumed with the state of Ginny's injuries, I was easily distracted and pulled into the deep depths of the internet. I was quickly reminded of what a bad idea it was to search for medical information. Nearly every website predicted gruesome conclusions to brain injuries from gunshots. But this time, I was led to a report with a different ending. I found a news story about a thirteen-year-old boy who tried to commit suicide and was rushed to the hospital with a gunshot wound to his head. The medical report said that he had a long hospital stay, but in his three-month follow-up, he had shown "phenomenal recovery." His speech was slow and deliberate, but he answered questions appropriately and was able to tell jokes. Four months later, he returned to school in a regular classroom, received a small amount of special education support, and then continued to consistently score As and Bs.

I read the report to Grandma who sat across from me reading her Bible. She looked up and said, "Emily, that's God at work. He is the ultimate healer you know. Things that seem impossible to us are not with him. We just need a teeny tiny amount of faith. In fact, the Bible says the amount is just the size of a mustard seed. Have you seen how tiny that is?"

I shook my head, knowing that as quick as she trotted away, she would return with a mustard seed to show me. I now knew Grandma had nearly every piece of the natural world in her house somewhere.

"Look at this," she said. She held up a silver chain with a clear pendant hanging from it. I reached for the pendant and looked closer. A tiny brown fleck rested inside. "That little thing is a mustard seed," she said. "That's the amount of faith you need. God is big enough to take this tiny seed and cause it to bloom into all those yellow mustard flowers we see all over the hills. Once those mustard flowers start to spread, it's almost impossible to stop them. Isn't that beautiful? I look at those yellow hills in a different way ever since I learned that."

Just like all the other nature items she talked about, I knew I would look at mustard differently too, probably even the mustard I put on food. Once Grandma told her stories, they had a way of sticking.

"I think you should keep this," she said.

I didn't always want the things she gave me, but I had to admit this one was pretty cool. I smiled and took it from her. "Thanks Grandma." I went to bed that night with the necklace in my hand, and fell asleep to the thought of mustard flowers.

I had no interest in getting out of bed the next morning, especially since I didn't have to rush to get ready for school. But as usual, the smell of Grandma's cooking was enticing. It smelled like the apple and cinnamon muffins she made for us a few times already. Jared and I couldn't get enough of them. Every time she made them, we devoured them within a day. I was surprised she wasn't tired of making them for us.

I heard my phone beep. To my surprise, I had three missed calls and a voicemail from Mrs. Bartle. That feeling of panic crept over me again. Now getting up was not a problem. I bolted out of bed and ran to Jared's room.

"Jared, Jared wake up," I said as I stood up and shook him a little.

"What's up?" he said, opening his eyes wide and jolting up.

"Sorry, I hate to wake you, but Mrs. Bartle called us. I thought you might want to hear the voicemail with me."

I was actually pretty sure he didn't care about hearing it and would have been fine with me telling him what she said, but I didn't want to listen alone.

"Oh, yeah, sure. Go ahead and play it."

I tapped the play icon and took a deep breath. "Emily? This is Mrs. Bartle. Ginny is awake, and she's actually talking a little. She's asking about you. I don't know if you can make it back any time soon, but I thought you should know. I don't want you to think everything is fine. She's well, uh, not the same, but she's communicating. I don't even know how long it will last, but anyway, if you can come, that would be great. Thanks dear."

Once she hung up, I let out the breath I'd been holding. "Oh my gosh, this is such good news," I said. "I know you probably aren't up to another long drive, but I would love to see her, even if I only hear her mumble one word."

"Oh, I'm not in the mood to drive, but I can't imagine doing anything else today knowing that Ginny is talking and wants to see us. I'm ready whenever you are, Em."

I would have rushed away immediately to get ready if I wasn't so surprised by Jared's response, which wasn't the words he said. It was his hand, resting on top of mine, holding it tight, making me want to stay right there forever.

# —29—

I stared at our hands, soaking in the moment, then looked him in the eyes. There aren't many people I can lock eyes with and feel comfortable. I usually turn my gaze away after a second or two, but with Jared, it was never awkward. He looked at me and smiled, then squeezed my hand tight once again.

I squeezed back this time, and inhaled, "Okay, well, we should eat breakfast with Grandma, but I'm sure she'll understand if we have to make it quick to go see Ginny. So, we can eat, and then head over. I'll text Mrs. Bartle and let her know we're on our way."

Grandma was her usual self at breakfast. She hummed while she sipped her tea, added some leaves to the growing collection on the table, and then proceeded to chat about one of them while we ate those amazing muffins.

"Have you ever looked closely at all the lines on one little leaf?" She said as she held a tiny red leaf in her hands. There are so many of them, but the little ones all branch out from the bigger, main ones. They seem to need that big vein in order to even exist at all. And do you know what's so amazing about this one I found today?"

Jared and I looked up, our mouths full of crumbs. "Hmmm?" I managed to say.

"Look, right here in the center."

I looked where she was pointing, to a hole in the center of the leaf. It was a tiny heart, perfectly shaped as though someone had pressed one of those mini cookie cutters into it.

"Isn't that something?" she said. I could have walked right past it, stepped on it even. But something made me pay attention to it, and I know you might be sick of me saying stuff like this, but I can't help it. I think it's a little gift from God. I think there's a lot of those little gifts all around us every day that we simply don't see. Anyway, if one of you wants to take it with you today, please do. Maybe Mrs. Bartle would like it, or maybe even Ginny. It reminds me that God is right in the center of everything. We're like all these little leaf lines and he's right there with us. We just need to pay attention."

Grandma's talks had begun to make more sense to me, and I didn't know if that was because her stories had become better or if I was becoming more used to them. Either way, I liked them.

"I'd love to take it, Grandma," I said. "Ginny and her mom would both like it."

I took the leaf and admired it while we finished eating. When we left, I took it with me and held it on the drive, rubbing my fingers over the edges of the heart shape, remembering what Grandma said. *God is in the center of everything. He's right here with us. He's right with Ginny. She's going to be okay.*

I was so excited to see Ginny, but I was also afraid of what I might see. I was so used to the spunky, witty, talkative girl. I didn't know what I might do if she was struggling to speak, if she was sad or in pain.

"I'm kind of scared to see her," I admitted to Jared.

He glanced over at me and said, "Yeah, I know, me too. It's hard to imagine her laying in a hospital bed struggling to speak. But it really is amazing she's talking at all. If she's already asking for us, it can only get better, right?"

"Yeah, I think so." I continued to stare at the leaf. It made me feel better about all this.

"Thanks for driving to see her again. I feel bad that I'm always bugging you to help me. I know it's a hassle, and eats up all your gas, but I'd hate to do this without you."

He looked at me again and took a deep breath. He said nothing, looked in the rearview mirror behind him, then veered off the road and put his hazard lights on.

What was he doing? Why was he pulling over? "Is everything okay?" I asked.

He glanced at me again. He looked nervous. "I just want you to know something, Em."

"Okay," I grasped the leaf, preparing myself for whatever was about to come my way.

"So, I don't do these things with you because I think I have to. I don't drive hundreds of miles to see your mom or Ginny because you make me. I don't sleep in a shoebox of a room on a bed that's sized for a five-year-old and wake up happy because of a good sleep. I like being with you, Em, and even though I get bummed sometimes about my dad not being around, the fact is, he wasn't real great to be around a lot of the time. The one good thing he did after my mom died was date your mom, but as great as I always thought your mom was, I really wasn't thrilled when they got engaged. I was actually sort of angry because that took any chances of dating you out of the picture if we were going to be brother and sister. It sucks to have my dad in jail, even though he deserved it. But maybe the one good thing about it is there's little chance our parents are going to get married now. So, yeah, maybe this isn't the time to tell you all this, but it's been bugging me for a while, so there it is."

Wow, I didn't expect that. I always knew he cared about me, but I didn't know it was like this. I didn't know he had a crush on me.

When I looked at Jared, I saw something I hadn't seen yet.

He looked afraid, but not the same way I'd seen before, not the way he looked when Ginny was shot or when the police came to our house that horrible morning. He looked insecure, like he wondered if he'd said something he shouldn't. It was the way I felt most of the time, wondering what people thought of me. I'd never seen Jared like that before. He always seemed so confident, so sure of himself.

"Jared, I've had a crush on you pretty much since the day I met you. Brit and I used to talk about it all the time, and laughed about how horrible it would be once your dad and my mom married because then I'd end up having you for a brother."

His smile returned, his shoulders relaxed.

"And even if your dad wouldn't have gone to jail, the marriage would have been off. I didn't tell you something my mom told me when I saw her. She told me the engagement with Richard was off. I've been so focused on Ginny, I didn't think to bring it up, but that's probably why he took you. He figured he'd take you and run with no reason to stay here anymore."

Jared looked like a light turned on, like he understood something. "Ah, yep, that makes sense. He was really upset, I mean, more than normal. I kept asking him why he had this sudden desire to leave California, why he wouldn't take you with us, not that you'd want that. I asked him if he'd said goodbye to your mom. I asked where we were going, if we were coming back. He never gave me answers. He told me to stop asking so many questions and to trust that he was doing what was best for us. I could go ask him now if I had any interest in visiting him in jail, but I don't think it matters. He probably wouldn't tell me the truth anyway."

That was accurate. Lies were the one thing I'd learn to count on with Richard. "All that matters is that he isn't getting away with all his cheating and lies and crimes anymore, and I know you love him still. He's your dad and that will never change. But I'm glad he didn't take you away, and I'm glad the police caught him."

"Me too, Em. I wish he was a different person. I wish he was that dad I always hoped he'd become. But that's not gonna happen."

As much as I disliked Richard, hearing Jared say that felt wrong. If I stopped hoping my mom would get better, I'd feel horrible.

"I wouldn't give up on that hope, Jared. Maybe prison will change him. Maybe incarceration is the horrible thing that will finally make things better for both our parents. I don't think I can control when my mom gets out, and I don't think she's innocent anymore, but I do think she can get better."

"Maybe," he sighed, then reached out to grab my hand. "But whether they change or not isn't going to keep me from being happy anymore. So what do you say, since you're not going to be my stepsister, will you go to prom with me, Emily Greene?"

I had to restrain myself from jumping out of my seat to hug him. The idea of being more than friends had been forced out of my mind for so long. Pretending I didn't like him had been one of those things that dragged me down. Hearing him ask me to prom reminded me that maybe something in my life could be normal. Everything didn't have to be sad. Things could get better.

"Sure, I'll go to the prom with you, Jared."

That confident smile returned to his face, beaming right through to my heart.

# –30–

Once I'd said yes, a million thoughts went through my head, like what if dating Jared didn't work? If things were ruined, would I lose my best friend? Also, as excited as I was to go to prom next Saturday, I couldn't help but think about how excited Ginny was to go, and now she wouldn't have the chance. Then I remembered a story I saw on the news a while back, where friends of a girl who was in the hospital for cancer treatments decided to bring the school dance to her.

"Jared, I have an idea," I said, wondering if he would swerve off the road again once I told him my plan.

"Uh-oh, do I need to pull over? At the rate we're going, we'll see Ginny at midnight. You have that sound in your voice that comes whenever you're thinking of something a little crazy."

"Okay, well, maybe it's crazy, but it's good, and no, keep driving. You can handle it."

He laughed, glanced over at me with one eyebrow raised, like he wasn't so sure of that.

"What if we took the money we would spend on prom tickets and put it towards bringing prom to Ginny in the hospital? I really want to go to prom, but she's been bugging me to go, with you in fact, and I kept telling her no. I figured you'd be going with someone else."

Jared laughed, "That's funny, Em. Who would I go with? You do realize my entire social life has been basketball. I have no idea if any of the team is even going. It's not really something we talk about at practice or games, which is the only time I see them."

I realized that was true. I couldn't picture them tossing the ball around, chatting about what kind of tux they would wear. "Yeah, I get that, but the girls always stare at you, Jared. One of them probably would ask you."

"I think they stare at me because I'm new. They stare at you too, Em, probably because they're jealous."

Now I laughed. "Very funny, they have nothing to be jealous over. They really hate me for some reason, which is one reason I didn't want to go to prom without a group of people or a date."

"They don't like you because you're a threat. They don't want you stealing the attention of their boys. You shouldn't even care what they think, Em. Let 'em stare and talk smack all they want. They'll give up when they see it's not getting to you."

I knew he was right. I'd heard this before. I thought back to the last time Ginny asked if I was going to prom. It was on our way to visit Mom in jail, the wrong time to ask me about something that would make my life feel even more depressing. After I told her I didn't want to go because I wasn't in the mood to have people talk behind my back, call me Jail Baby, her response was, "Emily, haven't you heard the expression 'sticks and stones will break your bones, but names will never hurt you?'"

"Yes," I told her, "I have heard that, but those idiots did more than say mean words. They planted drugs in my backpack and got me suspended. So sometimes words also come with horrible actions, and they do hurt." I then proceeded to tell her about the many times words had hurt me before. One of the times I told her about was the first day of school when I was in sixth grade. It was morning recess when Kiera Smight, the girl everyone wanted to be, with perfect, long, glossy blonde hair and perfect grades and perfect coordinating outfits from Forever 21 or Abercrombie, stood in front of me on the sand, arms crossed, chomping gum loudly but still looking perfect, and said, "Where'd you get that get-up? Did your mom sew it for you?"

I was crushed. The fact was, my mom had made it for me, which I hadn't been ashamed of until that very moment. We didn't have a lot of money, but Mom wanted me to have new clothes for school. We drove to the fabric store and picked out a pattern. It was a pair of pants with a matching vest and a button down blouse. I knew no one would find anything in the stores as cool as that. Nearly every minute for two weeks that my mom wasn't working, she was sewing. When I finally tried it on, I loved it. I paired it with a pair of my favorite boots and couldn't wait to show it off. Apparently, Kiera, the one I thought would love it most, thought it was horrible.

"I can't believe you think that looks good. You look like a dumb cowgirl or something." She laughed, and her posse of friends laughed with her.

"Howdy, Cowgirl!" Macy Walters shouted.

"Yee-haw!" another girl yelled, starting a chant of "yee-haws" that continued every time they passed me that day.

Ginny actually laughed when I told her that. "Okay, that's kind of funny, sorry. You shouldn't have let her get to you. When people say mean things to me, I don't let them hurt me anymore. It only hurts if you let their words speak louder than what you think about yourself, and if they see you're not bothered, they eventually shut up. You should have told her your family owned a ranch with horses. You could have totally made her jealous and had all the other girls wanting to be your friend so they could see your horses, which you could totally get out of by telling them your horses didn't like mean girls."

That was Ginny, the first responder everyone needed in mean girl emergencies like these. I wished I had her for a friend back then. I might have done what she said, or maybe I would have worn that outfit all the time and shouted "Yee-haw!" back at them without a care. I hoped that bringing the prom to Ginny would be one way I could help her for a change.

At the hospital, Jared grabbed my hand and we walked in proudly through the hospital doors.

"You okay?" Jared asked before we entered her room.

"Yeah, I am, thanks," I said, meaning it for the first time in a while.

That great Ginny smile I saw when we strode into her room made me forget there was anything wrong with her. She had a million wires and tubes attached to her, but she saw me and her eyes opened wider, her smile even bigger.

"Ginny, oh my gosh, hi," was all I could say as I dashed to her side and leaned in to hug her.

"E . . . Em . . . i . . . ly," she forced out. So, my fears of her not being able to speak the same were true, but it didn't matter to me anymore. I was thrilled to hear her at all. I pulled away and looked at her. "I . . . I . . . thought Richard shot y . . . y . . . you." She stopped and took a breath. "B . . . b . . . but I . . . I . . . guess it w . . . w . . . was o . . . o . . . on . . . ly me."

Mrs. Bartle stood on the other side of the bed. "She's been so worried that you were hurt. She didn't believe me that you were fine. Thank you so much for coming."

"Oh, please don't thank me. I'm so glad to be here." I looked back to Ginny. "I'm so happy to see you," I said, "and hear you."

"I . . . I . . . don't . . . talk . . . right," Ginny said.

"Ginny, the sound of your voice is beautiful. Don't worry. You'll get better. I know it." I held her hand.

Ginny glanced behind me, a huge smile on her face. "J . . .

J . . . J . . . Jared?"

"Hey, Ginny," he said. He leaned down and hugged her. "I'm so glad you're okay."

She smiled, nodded her head. It seemed like she had a million things she wanted to say, but didn't have the energy to do so.

"This is a lot of work for her, I'm sure," Mrs. Bartle said. "Do you want to rest up a bit, sweetheart?"

Ginny managed to cast that defiant look at her mom I'd seen before. "M . . . M . . . Mom, nnnnno."

"Okay, okay, just checking." She patted her hand and sat back down in the chair next to her.

"We have some fun news for you, Ginny," I said.

She looked up at me with wide eyes, her brows raised.

"Jared and I are going to the prom. So, you won't be going alone with Chris. We are going to have that amazing time you talked about."

Ginny smiled wide, but her eyes filled with tears.

"I . . . I . . . I d . . . d . . . don't." She exhaled, then took in another deep breath. Tears rolled down her cheeks now. "Can't g . . . g . . . g . . . go." She rested her head back, wiped her tears, kept her eyes shut.

This was not the reaction I expected. I didn't mean to make her sad.

"Emily, I think she isn't sure if she will feel up to it. When is it, again?" Mrs. Bartle asked.

"It's next Saturday," Jared said. "But we didn't mean to upset her. We actually had an idea we'd like to tell her about, right Em?"

"Yes, Ginny, we do. We talked about prom on the way here, and we decided that it's not really going to be a fun prom without you. So, we need to check with the hospital, but we'd like to bring prom here to you, or wherever you are, just you, me, Jared, and Chris. Would you like that?"

Her eyes popped wide open and she sat up abruptly. "Wh . . . wha . . . what? Ye . . . ye . . . yes!"

"Okay, then. We'll start getting it together. I know you've got your dress already. Is it a problem to get it here, Mrs. Bartle?"

She shook her head, smiling through her tears. "Oh no, it's not a problem at all. This is so wonderful. I am happy to get her dress, and honestly, I can arrange everything with the hospital. It's a long trip back and forth here to try to talk to people, and I'm here every day. I know who to talk to."

I tucked my hair behind my ear with hesitation. "That seems like an awful lot for you to do, Mrs. Bartle. I hate to drop more onto your plate.

"Emily, it makes me so happy to be able to do something for you all, really. So, as long as you don't mind me bothering you all with advice on music and décor and stuff, I'd really love to do it. Please, let me do this for you."

I could tell she meant it, and I got the feeling this would be something that would make her feel like she could finally do something to help Ginny. That's how I felt about it too.

"Okay, that would be great, Mrs. Bartle," I smiled up at her and squeezed Ginny's hand, feeling so thankful this would work.

"Yeah, it really would, and as far as advice goes, I think you've got the expert right here with you." Jared nodded over to Ginny.

She smiled, put a thumb up and smiled.

I reached into my purse, thinking this might be the perfect time for the leaf. "My grandmother also has a surprise for you. But as you'd imagine, it's much simpler than prom."

I took the leaf and held it up. "A leaf, hooray!" I cheered sarcastically.

Ginny smiled at me the way she does when she thinks I'm acting strange, which in this case was quite appropriate.

"I know. You're used to hearing me complain about the

stories behind all the stuff my grandmother finds. But I don't know, I think I'm starting to like them. Here's what she said about this. Do you see the heart shape in the center of the leaf?"

I held it closer to both Ginny and her mom.

"Yes, I do," Mrs. Bartle said.

"Mmhmm," Ginny nodded.

"Well, my grandmother said it reminds her of how God is at the center of everything. She found this today, and said most people walk right past things like this. We don't notice all the little gifts God gives us when we don't pay attention."

Ginny kept smiling at me, but no longer like she thought I was acting strange, more like she knew exactly what I meant.

"I would absolutely have to agree with that, Emily," Mrs. Bartle said. "You know, a lot of people say your grandmother is crazy. Even I have wondered that. Well, if crazy is the word to describe someone who says things like that, then crazy has a whole new meaning. Those are the most sound words I've heard in a while."

That was the first time I'd heard that spoken about my grandmother.

"Yeah, I think you're right," I replied.

I finally felt proud to be related to that Crazy Carol.

# –31–

When I was younger, maybe six or seven, I loved playing dress up. I would rummage through my mom's closet on Saturday mornings while she slept, selecting shoes first. I'd slip my feet into a pair of heels and then hobble around feeling transformed into adulthood. Then I'd wrap a scarf around my neck, and occasionally, I'd manage to pull a dress off a hanger and pull it over my head. A short dress for my mom was a long gown for me. If I found a handbag, I'd grab that, and then off I'd go to my room where I could pretend to shop, or work, or dine at a fancy restaurant.

Now that prom was a certainty, dress up took on a new meaning. Now it was real, and even though it was at the hospital, it was still my first real date, and I wanted the perfect dress. It wasn't the first time I thought about what I would wear to prom. I had some practice while shopping with Ginny for her dress the day after we'd gone out for pizza.

"You have to try this on." Ginny had said while holding up a skinny black dress.

"Uh, why would I try that on? I'm not going to prom."

"You don't know that yet. There's still time. Come on, what else do you have to do while I shop? This would look so cute on you. Just try it for fun." She shoved the dress at me.

I rolled my eyes at her, but grabbed the dress and went into a dressing room. When I looked at myself in the mirror, I loved it. The fabric hugged close at the waist, but then flared out just enough at the hips to not feel too tight. It stopped just above my knees, and I stood on my toes to picture my legs in heels. I imagined what I could wear to add some sparkle, maybe a silver necklace or some teardrop earrings. Seeing myself in it made me wish I had a good reason to buy it.

"Oh my gosh, you have to get it. Just wear it to school Monday and boys will be fighting over who gets to ask you out first," Ginny said when she saw me in it. "How about I take a picture and Instagram it to all the boys I know?"

She went to grab her phone, but I yelled, "Ginny! No! I'm not letting you do that!" I did not want my picture all over social media. The last thing I needed was more opportunities for people to gawk at me. I ran back to my dressing room, latched the door, and quickly began to change.

"Whatever!" Ginny yelled through the door. "But I still think you should buy it!"

I didn't follow her advice, and sadly hung the dress back up, but not before I checked the price tag to see if it was even in the price range. It definitely was not. The small amount of money I had from babysitting back home and saving up Christmas gift money was not going to last long if I wasn't careful. Eighty-five dollars was at least fifty dollars out of the price range, which basically meant the only way I would get a prom dress (if I ended up going) was by thrift shopping or borrowing one, somehow.

The evening after we visited Ginny, we told Grandma about our idea to have prom at the hospital with Ginny.

"Well, that sounds absolutely wonderful, so thoughtful. And I don't mean to embarrass you, but are you two going as a date or as future brother and sister?" She looked at our hands, which we were holding together without really thinking about it.

"Oh, yeah, uh, we're going as a date," Jared smiled as he looked at me.

She looked at us with raised eyebrows, a swirl of questions clearly popping into her mind.

We told her what Mom had said about the engagement being off, which she probably assumed since Richard had been arrested. But we also explained how we were friends first, and that it never felt right that we were maybe going to go from that to stepbrother and stepsister if our parents married.

She thought about all that for a minute, and then said, "Okay, well, I guess I'd better keep a closer eye on you two now."

This was where the fact that Jared and I were such good friends came in handy. There weren't many things that embarrassed us. I smiled and rolled my eyes as Jared quietly laughed.

But Grandma wasn't letting our carefree attitude stop her from a teachable moment. "You know, when I was about your age, I liked a boy a lot. He was cute, and smart, and funny. That was your grandpa, Emily." She bobbed her tea bag up and down in her cup and gazed upward, smiled like she was imagining her younger love. But her dreamy face turned cautious when she said, "We got married when we were a bit too young. Your mom, she sort of did the same thing, not the marrying young part, but her and your dad got serious real fast, and things didn't work out. So, I'm not saying that's what will happen here, but don't rush into things. Be careful, okay?"

We both nodded our heads.

"We'll be careful," Jared said. "We've been friends for a long time. I wouldn't want to ruin that."

Grandma patted him on the cheek. "You're a nice boy, Jared. I'm glad you're in Emily's life."

"Thanks," Jared held Grandma's hand and smiled. "Me too."

"So, what are you going to wear, Emily? I don't know if you're interested, but I still have some dresses here your mom left behind. You look about her size if you want to try them."

The thought of trying on my mom's clothes again felt a little scary. While there were so many times I wanted something of hers to feel closer to her, sometimes they made me miss her more. Clinging to her things wasn't the same as clinging to her, and sometimes that was too painful to swallow.

"Um, okay, but I can probably find something at the thrift store in town," I said.

Grandma misunderstood my hesitation. "Oh, yes, I'm sure you could, dear. But you don't need to do that if you like what you see here. I'm sure your mom would love for you to wear one of her dresses. Come on, let's go take a look."

Before I could respond, Grandma hustled halfway down the hall. She moved fast when she was excited about something. I got up to follow her, and Jared grabbed my hand.

"Hey, are you okay?" he whispered. "You don't have to wear your mom's dress."

I loved that he knew what I was thinking.

"I know, thanks. I'm not sure how I feel about it. I'll go look and then decide."

He squeezed my hand gently, which gave me a surprising amount of strength to go down that hall. Grandma had already opened the closet, laid two dresses on the bed, and held one by the hanger, admiring it. It was the one from the picture, a long narrow black dress, a lot like the one I had tried on with Ginny that day, only longer, and already accessorized with the sparkle the other one missed. The neckline had a shimmery silver trim that continued along delicate spaghetti straps, and around the hanger was a silver necklace strung with clear glass beads and tiny black gems.

I reached out and felt the fabric, soft, silky. "It's really pretty," I said. "It reminds me of one I tried on with Ginny. I loved it, but I could never afford it, and it actually wasn't even as pretty as this one."

I didn't tell her how awed I felt that Mom had created a dress just like the one I would want to wear, another reminder of how alike we were.

"Your mom had good fashion sense and a knack for making beautiful things. We didn't have a lot of money for clothes, but she could take a scrap of bargain priced fabric and create a masterpiece."

That sounded like the mom I knew. I hoped *that* mom was still there somewhere.

"Do you want to try it on?" Grandma asked.

I hesitated, kept looking at it and picturing Mom in it, wishing she were the one holding it, smiling and eager for me to wear it, telling me all about what prom was like for her. I didn't want to cry about this. I was so tired of crying over stuff I couldn't do anything about, but those stupid tears came anyway.

"Oh, dear, I'm sorry. I've upset you with this. I didn't mean to, but I wasn't thinking. Let's put it away. We'll find you something to wear that's even better."

She pulled the dress away and turned to put it back in the closet, but seeing her do that made me want it back. I craved that piece of my mom that was once happy, carefree, in love.

"No, it's okay," I said, wiping my tears. "I want to try it. It just made me miss her. That's not your fault."

Grandma slowly turned back around with the dress in hand. "Are you sure? I understand why this would be difficult, and you shouldn't feel sad about the dress you wear to prom."

"I'm sure, Grandma."

Grandma gave me the dress and walked toward the door. "You let me know if you want me to see you in it. I'm going to go make some tea," she said.

I doubted she really wanted more tea after the three cups she'd already drank, but I appreciated her excuse to give me some privacy.

I took my time changing. I held the dress in front of me first and looked in the mirror, then took the necklace off and let it glide through my fingers.

"Okay, here goes," I said like I was about to jump off a cliff or something.

Once I pulled the dress on and clasped the necklace behind my neck, I waited to look into the mirror and walked to the desk where the picture of my mom and dad smiled back at me. I was always told I looked like my mom, and the younger version of her was even more of a match. I held the picture in my hands and ran my fingers along her face. It radiated pure joy. And my dad, that man I still had only seen in pictures, beamed like the luckiest man on earth.

I kept the picture in my hand as I walked back to the mirror. I kept my gaze down and stared at my mom one more time before I slowly let my eyes look into the mirror, at my toes barely peeking out from the hem, to my waist, to my neck beneath the glistening beads, and finally to my face that so clearly resembled the young Tiffany. I had felt afraid to see her in me again. But it felt okay. This dress reminded me of the good in her. Like this beautiful dress that hung for years in the closet, that good didn't have to hide forever. It could still come out and shine like it did before.

# –32–

"Okay, I'm wearing it!" I shouted out the bedroom door.

Grandma's feet pattered down the hall quicker than I'd ever heard before.

"Oh my," was all she said, but her hands over her mouth and the tears in her eyes said much more than that.

"You look just like her," she brushed away a tear.

This was probably as difficult for her as it was for me.

"Yeah, I do." I glanced at her picture again.

Grandma reached out for it. I handed the frame to her, and she did the same thing as me, ran her fingers over it, shook her head in slight disbelief, like she was thinking about that girl she once knew.

"She was so happy that day," Grandma said. "Your parents were simply giddy over each other."

"It shows," I said, wondering how they went from that to not even speaking to each other. It especially didn't make sense based on Grandma's story of how my dad really seemed to want to talk to my mom. Maybe he also wanted to talk to me. Maybe he always wanted a relationship with me, but never had a chance.

"Grandma, do you think my father would talk to me if I reached out to him? Do you know where he is? Do his parents still live out here, like you?"

Grandma stared at me a bit, nodded her head. "They live in the same house your father grew up in. I run into them every once in a while, but we don't say much to each other. It's a bit awkward actually. I've always felt like they're upset with me for raising a daughter who broke things off with their son. That may not be true, but I still feel a bit uncomfortable around them."

I could understand that. They might not want anything to do with me either, but I felt like I needed to try.

"I might be crazy to ask for this, but do you think you could take me to their house? Maybe they can help me get in touch with my dad."

Grandma breathed in deep, then let it out. "I can do that. I think it's very brave of you and also important. If there's a chance at having a relationship with your dad, it's worth trying. I don't know how they could look at their beautiful granddaughter and not help."

"Thanks, Grandma," I said.

I heard Jared walking down the hallway. "Hey, do I get to see the dress?"

I didn't know why he bothered asking when he was already at the door, his head peering in.

"It looks like you are seeing it," I laughed.

"Wow." His eyes opened wide. Like grandma, he didn't say anything else right away, but his expression told me more. This was quite a switch from my usual sweatshirt and jeans.

"You think it's okay?" I asked to make sure I wasn't reading him wrong.

"You look amazing. It doesn't look like some old dress I pictured in my mind. It's perfect."

"Okay then. I guess now the pressure's on you to match me."

"Oh, that's not too hard," Grandma said. "Tuxedos are always available, and they match any dress. There's a rental shop in town by the grocery store."

"Yep, I've seen it, and I'm glad your dress is black. I'm not sure I'd want to wear a bright pink or green bow tie like some guys do to match the girl's dress. I'd do it for you, Em, but still."

"Oh, well, just because I'm wearing a black dress, doesn't mean you can't have a splash of color, Jared."

"No, no, I'm good, thanks though," he replied.

I was so happy to be doing this prom thing with him. I was so glad to be with someone who laughed with me, understood me, let me be me.

After he left the room, Grandma held my hand and said, "You let me know when you want to go to the Sharpes' house. I can take you whenever you feel up to it."

It felt strange to know I had another set of grandparents nearby who I'd never met, two people related to me by blood, but removed from me by choices I never made.

"Maybe we could go after school tomorrow?" I asked.

"Sure, that sounds good. I'll pick you up and we can go from there."

After she left the room, I changed out of the dress and hung it carefully. I then flipped through a few more items of my mom's in the closet. There were still sweaters and jackets of hers, including an old high school sweatshirt. Maybe I could wear that on a spirit day, I joked to myself, knowing that I had absolutely no desire to show any school spirit for that miserable place. Then I thought of what was happening after school the next day, and I suddenly thought maybe I didn't even want to get out of bed tomorrow. I was excited to have a chance to talk to my grandparents, but I also worried they'd want nothing to do with me and wouldn't help me see my dad.

I lay down and closed my eyes. I tried to picture what my grandparents would look like and how they would react to some stranger on their front step. I hated answering the door when I didn't know who was on the other side. I never could understand why people went house to house asking for things.

They'd have to be okay with a lot of rejection. I hoped that wouldn't be what I got tomorrow.

I imagined a couple with gray hair, looking at me like I was another teen wanting money for some school fundraiser. What would they say when I said who I was? How would I even say it? Would I simply blurt out, "Hello, I'm your granddaughter, nice to meet you; can you help me talk to my dad?" Would they look at me with annoyance like they didn't want to be bothered? Would they actually prefer that I was that unknown kid asking them to donate money for high school band camp or whatever sports team they were on? Did they know Mom was in jail, and I was living with Grandma? If so, why hadn't they tried to meet me?

My head swirled with all these questions, all these doubts that made me want to run in and tell Grandma I'd changed my mind. Was it really that important to me to talk to my dad?

My anxious thoughts were interrupted by a knock on my door.

"Hey Em, can I come in?" Jared said.

"Yeah, sure," I said. I opened my eyes and sat up as he came in.

"Oh, sorry. Were you sleeping? I didn't mean to bug you."

"No, it's okay. I was just thinking. I don't think I could sleep now if I wanted to."

"Yeah, I hear you're going to talk to your dad's parents tomorrow. That sounds like fun."

I knew he was being sarcastic. He knew how huge this was for me. "Jared, what if they want nothing to do with me? What if they won't help me talk to my dad?"

"Well, I don't think that'll happen, but if it does, there are other ways we can find your dad, and it's their loss if they don't help you. They're missing out on getting to know a really great girl."

His words meant a lot to me. I hoped he was right.

Jared must have sensed my doubt lingering. "I know my situation isn't exactly the same, but I've always known my dad didn't really want anything to do with me. I mean, he did if it helped him somehow, but he didn't want to just be with me because I was his son, you know?"

I nodded. I knew how selfish Richard was. "So, how are you so confident? You don't seem to get too worried about whether people like you or not."

He smiled, "Yeah, well, I do, but I don't let it take over me. Instead, I think about what my mom would say about me, what she would tell me whenever someone hurt my feelings or whenever I was sad about my dad.

"What did she say?"

"She'd tell me that no matter what anyone says, I was created perfectly. She told me God doesn't make mistakes, so if someone makes fun of me or is being mean to me, they're basically making fun of God."

I had never thought of things that way. "Wow, that's good. I see who you get your smarts from."

"Yep, Richard and I are one and the same."

There he was, always finding a way to lighten things up. "Very funny," I said with a laugh. "But seriously, I'm hanging on to your mom's words. And the funny thing, they kind of sound like something my grandma would say."

"Yeah, they do. That must be why I like your grandma. That and the fact that she feeds us really well."

"No kidding," I said, remembering the meatloaf and mashed potatoes I inhaled at dinner.

We could hear her in the kitchen, clanging dishes in the sink as she cleaned them. And above that, as always, we could hear her voice, singing a song I'd heard her sing many times before, but this time, the words spoke straight to my heart.

"I praise you because I am fearfully and wonderfully made; your works are wonderful, I know that full well."

I was beginning to think God might actually be speaking to me, that he probably had been all along, and now I was finally listening.

# –33–

I would never go to the extreme of saying I love school, but there had always been certain things about it I liked—seeing my friends, reading a cool story, learning some fun fact, actually understanding a math problem. But this day, I had a hard time finding anything positive. I mostly wanted to fast forward through everything so I could get to the part where I'd meet my grandparents. Time is painfully slow whenever there's something to be excited about. So ten minutes in, I was dying, and after six hours, I was about to explode.

Adding to my stress was the fact that it was my first day of track practice. Even though my last coach ran us to the point of begging for no more miles or no more intervals, it was usually my best part of a school day. There was something oddly satisfying about running to exhaustion with friends who were dying along with me. But today I didn't have any friends on the track team, and I knew it wouldn't feel the same, especially if my ankle started acting up. I also knew everyone would be watching me, judging whether I was good enough or worse, too good. The best runners might not want someone to take the spotlight away from them.

I moved quickly in the locker room, avoiding eye contact with anyone, hoping the girls next to me who were laughing loudly and blurting out inside jokes wouldn't notice me. After stepping into my running shorts and pulling on my blandest, least attention-grabbing gray T-shirt, I slipped on my running shoes. After tying them, I took a glance inside my track bag at the old shoes I took to every track event. They were my only source of comfort right now. They reminded me of what mattered to me, that I could win even when it was hard. No mean person on this team could steal that from me. I zipped up my bag, locked it in the locker, and without even thinking, said in my mind, *please walk past these girls with me, God.*

I stepped past them, saw one girl with long brown hair look up from tying her shoes, "Hey," she said with a casual smile, and then continued tying as if I was no big deal. Since I was so worried about being glared at, her simple acknowledgment felt like a huge answer to prayer.

Once I was on the field, it was like going home. We did the same warm-ups I'd done at every practice I'd had since seventh grade—high knees and butt-kicks, toe touches and runners' lunges, two laps around the track. Then we sat on the grass to stretch some more while waiting for our coaches to tell us what to do next.

A tall, lanky, dark-haired man spoke first. "Okay, so most of you know me, Coach Tino. Anyone who's a distance runner should come with me. That includes anyone who runs a 400 meter or more. I know a 400 is a sprint, but today we're conditioning to have speed and endurance, and for that race you need both, so you come with me."

I waited for a second for others to get up first, as I didn't want to call more attention to myself than necessary. I was glad to see the girl who had smiled at me get up, along with some of the other girls I recognized from my quick pass through the locker room. I got up and followed.

As we walked, Coach Tino strutted backward, taking inventory of his followers. "Lexi, good to see you joining me today," he said to the nice girl from the locker room. Now I at least knew her name. "Sean, nice to see you too," he said to one of the boys who towered over everyone, long and thin, proudly wearing the fashion statement of a bright green bandana around his forehead. Coach Tino then looked at me, much longer than he had with anyone else, obviously trying to figure out who I was.

"So you must be the new girl, Emily?"

So much for avoiding attention. Everyone turned to stare at me.

"Uh, yeah, that's me."

"Nice to meet you, Emily." He stopped and reached out his arm to shake hands. "I hear you're a promising 800 runner. We could always use one of those. We all seem to be afraid of that race, right folks?"

A number of responses blasted from that question.

"Coach Tino, that's because you ask us to run it along with the mile and the 400 and we're dead tired from those," Lexi pulled her long hair up and tied it into a ponytail.

"And you always make the 800 racers run more. Your workout nearly killed me the day I told you I was thinking about running it," Sean slowed down a little as he reached one arm over his head and pulled it back with the opposite hand to stretch his triceps. But even at a slower walk, I noticed that one of his strides equaled two of mine. That would definitely help his 800 time, even without conditioning for it.

"Yeah, I'm not doing it after seeing that brutality in action," said a guy with chin length wavy hair trotting to keep up with Sean.

Lexi looked to me and said, "I guess you're our hero, Emily. We will gladly cheer you on as Coach T imparts his torture for greatness method of training. He only needs one devoted follower and he's happy. Thanks for saving us."

I thought it was pretty cool the way they could jokingly refuse their coach's request to run a certain race. My coach back home never gave us much choice, and we didn't have different plans for the 800 runners. All the distance people pretty much did the same workout.

"Oh, congratulations, folks. Your winning attitudes have earned you one of my great lectures."

A series of groans and laughs followed, but that didn't stop him, and in spite of their negative reactions, they all stopped and looked interested.

"So, whether you're running an 800, or a mile, or a marathon, I'm going to push you. You know why?"

"Because you want us to be our best," they said in unison, some more enthusiastically than others.

"That's right. I want you to be your best. Not because we need to win a meet. Not because it matters what place you come in. But because if you can push it out here, you can push it in life. What you learn out here about challenge, hard work, giving it your all when you think you have nothing left, is going to transfer out there, off the track. And that matters. You hear me?"

"Yes Coach T," They said all together again.

"What's that? I didn't hear some of you."

"Yes, Coach T!" Everyone shouted this time, including me.

"Okay then, so what do you do when things get tough?"

"Keep going," a few said with the enthusiasm I knew wouldn't satisfy him.

"What? Can I hear that again? From everyone? Loudly? When things get tough, you what?" He stared at us with such intensity I couldn't even consider not responding.

"Keep going!" We all shouted loud enough to make me want to put my hands to my ears.

"Yes! That's right!" he yelled back. "Now we're ready to run some intervals. Let's go!" He jogged away, while everyone followed, and Sean quietly said, "Oh no, that speech means this is going to be a tough day."

He was right about that. We started with a six-mile run on

the streets, followed by eight 400 meter runs, six 100 meter sprints, and then a half-mile cool down and stretch. If his 800 runners had to normally do more than this, I was truly afraid. I couldn't imagine doing more. I was absolutely dead, my ankle throbbed, my whole body felt like rubber. Yet, I couldn't stop smiling. My mind felt free when I ran, and when I wore myself out, whatever I was uptight about seemed more tolerable. It was how I had survived living with Richard.

"Okay, athletes," Coach Tino announced. "You are officially all prepared for the 800 now. That's my best 800 training yet."

We were all flat on our backs, not wanting to move.

"You have got to be kidding me!" Lexi yelled. "You just put us all through an 800 athlete's training? That is so unfair."

Coach T laughed. "Yes, I did, Lexi. But the thing is, it's also a perfect training for any distance runner. So, yeah, it is fair. You guys can groan here a while longer if you need to, but I've gotta go do my own workout now. So, I'll see you guys tomorrow. Good job today."

He took off running around the track while none of us budged.

"Does someone want to carry me?" Sean pleaded.

"Yes, Emily does," Lexi announced. "Right Emily? You're the 800 runner, so you should be fine, right?" She looked over at me with a smile.

"Uh, no, definitely not," I muttered back with the remaining ounce of energy I had left. "But thanks for your confidence in me."

That was the other thing I'd missed about running, being around people who were more like me. Maybe I could make friends here. Maybe things would get better. And Coach T was right about one thing. That fight that I managed to find in me on that last interval was getting me through my next battle off the track, the next thing I was afraid to do—surprise my estranged grandparents with the gift of me.

# 34

Grandma and I sat in the car in front of the Sharpes' house with its white picket fence and cute green mailbox with a little iron horse on the top. Their home seemed too perfect, kind of intimidating. I had more motivation to move after my track workout than I did at that moment. I was pretty sure Grandma wasn't thrilled either, since she'd said it felt awkward whenever she ran into the Sharpes. But Grandma didn't let her insecure feelings take control. She acted brave as ever.

"You know we're not going up there alone, right?" Grandma said as she put her hand on mine.

I stared at her without responding, glanced at the street behind us to see if someone else was there. Grandma quickly cleared up my confusion.

"God is with us," she said as she reached for my hand. "He promises that. He doesn't say we'll have things easy, but he'll be right by our side through the tough stuff like this. So everything will be okay."

I nodded my head and tried to believe her. I was hoping I'd suddenly feel some powerful burst of courage. But I didn't. I remembered what Coach T said. If I could push through tough stuff on the track, I could push through in life.

"Okay, let's do this," I gave Grandma's hand a gentle squeeze and forced a smile.

We walked up the pathway that led us through a well-manicured lawn framed with yellow and purple flowers.

"Oh, look at those hydrangeas. They're beautiful. You know, I read once that the yellow ones are supposed to represent friendship and understanding. That's a good sign." She stopped and paused for a moment. "At least that's one theory. I also read that they stand for boastfulness or vanity. So, who knows? Good thing they're not in charge of the world." She waved her hand at them, like she was dismissing their worth, then started walking again. This actually made me laugh a little, making up for the fact that her inspirational messages weren't quite right today.

The door boasted a small Welcome sign on it, painted in green lettering with flowers the same colors as the ones we'd passed. This made me think they must be very particular about decor and how things looked. I wished I'd chosen a better outfit to wear.

Grandma took a deep breath, smiled at me, then pushed the doorbell. The ring made me jump a little inside like I did at the start of a race. There was no going back now, just all forward momentum. I heard talking. The door unlatched from the other side. Then it opened.

The man in the doorway, my grandfather, stood tall and stern. He looked at me first, a blank expression, and then at Grandma with surprise.

"Oh, Carol, hello. This is a surprise."

I could see why Grandma felt uncomfortable. He didn't seem to be real happy to see her. He had one hand on his hip, the other on the doorknob, eyes narrowed as he stared at us.

"Yes, hello Tom. I know you weren't expecting me."

A short, plump woman approached behind him. "Carol? Hello, how are you?" the lady said. She had a kind voice, and stood at least two feet below Tom. She dried her hands on the yellow apron tied around her waist. I could smell something like roast or soup from inside.

"I'm fine, thank you. I'm here to introduce you to someone I think you should meet."

Mr. Sharpe moved to the side so they both could get a look at me. Mr. Sharpe squinted his eyes and leaned forward to see me better. Mrs. Sharpe pulled her glasses down to the bridge of her nose, peered over them to eye me closely.

"There's no easy way to do this, so I'll just say it. This is your granddaughter, Emily, Landon's daughter."

They didn't move, kept their gaze straight on me, their mouths open as if something was about to come out but couldn't.

"My goodness . . . Emily." Mr. Sharpe stammered.

I stood there. On display. In the silence. Wishing to disappear.

"Please, Emily and Carol, come in. My goodness, no need for you to stand in the cold," Mrs. Sharpe said as she gently pulled Mr. Sharpe back to allow us to enter. A fire burned bright in the living room to our left. Fresh flowers and candles in crystal holders decorated a polished wooden coffee table. Dozens of silver-framed photographs were displayed on the end tables beside a green and gold paisley print sofa. I smelled warm soup cooking on the stove as we approached the kitchen.

"What can I get you two? Tea? Hot cocoa? A soda? What do you like? We have all kinds of things. Some oatmeal cookies maybe?" She bumped into a chair as she passed the kitchen table. I felt worse for her than myself now. She seemed so out of sorts, it hurt to watch. Discombobulated was the word that came to mind. I somehow remembered it from a vocabulary quiz back in Seventh Grade. I never thought I'd use it, but here it was, finding a place in my cluttered head. Nothing should have surprised me anymore.

Grandma looked at me with a slight smile that told me she also sympathized with Mrs. Sharpe.

"We don't need anything, Ruth. Please don't go to any trouble. We know this isn't something you were prepared for. Thank you for welcoming us so kindly," Grandma's voice sounded peaceful, but I knew she was nervous by the way she held her hands together, her fingers intertwined as if in prayer mode.

Her words brought a sense of calm. Mrs. Sharpe stopped mid flurry and took a deep breath. I could see some anxiety drain from her face.

"Oh, well, you're welcome, and yes, this is a bit of a surprise." She held her glance on me. "But a good one, Emily. We've often wondered about where you are and how you're doing, and when we heard the news about Tiffany, we didn't know how to get involved. We didn't think interfering would be helpful. But we are so glad you've come here to meet us."

I wasn't sure how to leap to the fact that I wasn't there simply to meet them. I focused my eyes on Mrs. Sharpe's smile and said, "Thank you, Mrs. Sharpe. It's really nice to meet you, and actually, there is something you could do."

"Oh yes, what is it?" She said as she leaned toward me like she was waiting for some big secret or announcement.

"Well, I'm hoping I can get in touch with my dad."

Mr. Sharpe still seemed on mute, and uncomfortable, forcing a smile that looked like the kind I probably made when Coach Tino told us to run our last interval with a better attitude. It wasn't a genuine grin, more of a turning up of lips with no joy behind it.

I noticed more framed photographs on the wall behind him, portraits of a boy I presumed was my father, and on the table below that, sat family pictures. A very recent picture of my father with a woman I'd never seen, and two young boys, caught my eye. Was that his new family? Did he have other children who he saw every day and a wife he loved?

Mr. Sharpe finally spoke. "We have a lot of pictures of your dad," he said. "But there's one that I really like that isn't out here. Come on, I'll show it to you."

He motioned for me to follow him. I really didn't want to see more pictures. I felt like I was about to cry. All this time I thought maybe my dad missed me, possibly wanted a daughter, but now I knew he had other children to love. I questioned if I still wanted to talk to him. Coach Tino's words echoed in my mind. *When things get tough, keep going. When things get tough, keep going.*

We entered a small room next to the living room that had some cluttered shelves and a desk. He opened the top drawer, rummaged through a pile of papers to find a blue envelope, and looked inside. "Yep, here they are. A couple of my favorites." He handed them to me.

On the top was the same photo from Mom's room, of her and my dad. Underneath that was another one of my teenage dad, sitting in a hospital room holding a baby. He looked down at that baby with a big smile. I rubbed my fingers over the photo, the same way I had with the other picture when I first saw it, as if doing so might bring me closer to him, to that day.

"That's me?" I said trying not to cry.

"Yep. The only picture I have of you. As hard as it was on your dad to have a kid so young, he was pretty happy that day he held you."

"It looks like he's still pretty happy," I said, hoping to hear more about his current family.

"Well, yes, he is. It took him a while to move on after your mother told him she wanted her space. He tried to stay in touch, but eventually he gave up. I don't know if that was the right thing to do, but it's what he chose." He breathed a deep sigh and looked me in the eye. "I showed you that picture so you'd know he cared about you, and I think he still does, but he's going to be surprised to hear from you."

"Yeah, I figured that. But I was hoping it would be a good

surprise. Now I'm not so sure. It looks like he's moved on, has another family of his own. I might be a problem now."

Mr. Sharpe nodded his head. "Emily, I can see why you'd think that. But you should never think of yourself as a problem because your parents made some mistakes. I'll be honest and tell you I'm not sure how your father will react. He might not be ready to talk to you." Mr. Sharpe glanced over at the photograph in my hand and continued. "He told us he had given up on you and Tiffany because it hurt too much to keep trying. So, he may try to protect himself and his current family. I'm not sure if Angeline, his wife, even knows about you. But still, you need to get in touch with him. He's your father. My relationship with him hasn't always been the best, and I regret that." He stopped, shook his head, swallowed hard as if trying to fight off the sadness he clearly felt, then looked me in the eyes. "So, you should do what you can. If he acts weird, it's not because of you."

I looked up at him and realized what we both had in common. We had both been broken. We both carried that around. My fear of meeting him and Mrs. Sharpe was silly. We were family, and even though we didn't know each other well, we still had a connection.

"Thank you, Mr. Sharpe."

"You're welcome, and you can call me Tom if you want. Around here I get called Big Tom a lot, not sure why. I'm not that big."

I laughed at that. Standing at least six foot five, he was probably the tallest person I'd ever met, one of those people where you look up and say to yourself, wow, he's tall. "Okay, Big Tom it is," I said. "And thanks for showing me these." I handed him the pictures and he smiled warmly as he took them from me.

"You're welcome," he said. "I guess we should go check on the ladies."

We returned to the living room where Grandma and Mrs. Sharpe stood talking and looking at the pictures on the wall. "He's such a handsome boy." I heard Grandma say.

Mrs. Sharpe smiled proudly and said, "Well, I think so too." When she noticed I'd returned, she said, "Emily, let me get that number for your father. He's in Pennsylvania, so you'll have to remember the time is three hours ahead of us here. I'll give you his cell phone number so you don't have to call the home number, and I'd call him during the day even though he's working. That's probably better than trying to reach him at home in the evening."

I figured she might be telling me that so I didn't call when he was around his family, which seemed like a good idea. "Okay, thank you," I replied.

Mrs. Sharpe scurried away, leaving the three of us with the heavy job of filling the empty space with small talk. Luckily, Grandma was good at that.

"Your flowers out front are lovely," she said.

"Oh, yes!" Mr. Sharpe said way too enthusiastically, probably because he was thankful someone said something.

Mrs. Sharpe returned and handed me a slip of paper with the name Landon, underlined, followed by the nine digits that would connect me to my father.

"Thank you," I said, feeling like I was holding the password to some top secret treasure.

"You're very welcome dear," she said as she grabbed my hands in hers and looked me in the eyes. "It really is so nice to finally meet you, Emily. I hope we can see you again, and if there's anything you need, please let us know." She squeezed my hand as a tear escaped her deep brown eyes.

"Thank you, Mrs. Sharpe, I will."

"Oh, and please call me Ruth. I know you won't want to call me Grandma right now, but no need to be formal."

I waited to hear if she also had a nickname, but if she did, she didn't mention it. I figured if she did it might be Real Ruth.

She seemed very genuine.

As we walked to the door, I turned to look one more time at that family photo of my dad and the siblings I always thought would be fun to have, but had now apparently taken my place. I hoped I wouldn't have to nickname him False Father, but I had a feeling that picture might be the truest form of him I'd get.

# –35–

It was 5:00 when we got back to Grandma's, which meant 8:00 in Pennsylvania. The advice to call my dad during the day replayed in my head. But with Grandma busy getting dinner ready and Jared still at practice, I couldn't focus on anything other than talking to my dad.

I didn't see how I'd manage to talk to him during the day anyway. I had school and track practice until four, so unless I woke up early and tried to call him before I went to school at 7:30, I didn't have a lot of options. Also, it wasn't really my problem or my fault that he might not have told his new family about me. I shouldn't feel guilty for being his daughter.

I took a deep breath and held it, then slowly let it out like I would on the starting line before a race. I picked up my phone, breathed deep again—in and out, and then pushed the numbers on my phone. The ringing sound that followed made my heart leap and beat fast. Part of me hoped for no answer, but then all my built-up fear would have been for nothing, all my courage wasted.

Then I heard it, his voice, in the cheerful tone of someone expecting a friendly and familiar voice on the other end. "Hello?" he said.

I froze. I couldn't get a single sound to come out. Stuck in my throat were so many words, so many thoughts. It was strange to me how that word, hello, so common, so frequent, suddenly meant a million little things to me. This one little word was about to open a closed part of my life, a window of truth about who my father was and what he thought about me.

I finally forced sounds out. "Hi, um, this is Emily."

No response. Silence followed for several seconds, and then he said, "I'm sorry, who?"

"Emily," I said, "your daughter, Emily Greene."

The pause that followed was way too long. Was he going to say something? Did I need to ask if he heard me? Was he still there?

"Oh, wow," was all that finally came after all that thinking time, followed by more nothingness, painful silence.

I was used to being the quiet one, used to the adults in my life taking charge and speaking. Maybe he was a quiet type too, maybe this was simply something we had in common and we'd eventually laugh about it. I couldn't wait any longer though, so I said, "I know this is a surprise."

"Uh, yes, it is. Wow, uh, I wasn't expecting this."

I wondered exactly how bad his social skills were. This was going nowhere. I scuffed my left foot across the hardwood floor, feeling sort of angry that he didn't even seem the slightest bit happy to hear from me. I figured I had nothing to lose, so I might as well speak my mind.

"I'm calling because I want to know the truth."

I waited a moment, hoping he might reassure me by saying he'd be honest with me, no matter what it was, but of course there was another awkward silence.

So, I continued, "Did you try to be in my life like my grandma tells me, or did you take off, not wanting anything to do with me, like Mom told me?"

I could hear someone in the background, a woman's voice. "Honey, who is it?" She shouted as if all his phone calls were for her too. I heard muffled whispers and pictured him covering the phone with his hand to answer her.

"Maybe we could meet and talk in person. I have plans to travel to California for business Thursday. Would that work for you?" He spoke to me like I was a client, all formal and fake. What's-her-face, Angelina, was probably in the room listening.

While I wished he had answered my question, I did want to meet him. "Uh, yeah, Thursday is fine," I said.

"Okay then, what's your address?" he asked, still sounding businesslike.

"Uh, I'm at Grandma's, Mom's old house, you know where that is?"

"Perfect, I know where that is. I have a morning flight and then I'll be done with my meeting around three. I'll be about three hours from you, so I can be there around six, okay?"

"Yeah, sure. That should be fine."

It seemed so strange to be setting a time and day to meet my father. It didn't seem like something that should exist in the world of appointment settings, but here I was, making it a thing and trying to pretend it was totally fine and normal, that he wasn't acting weird at all.

When I hung up the phone, I glanced at that one photo I had of him and took a deep breath. In approximately forty-eight hours I would meet the real live version of this person I was to call Dad.

# –36–

I paced back and forth in the living room, pressed my thumbs against each knuckle to crack them, jogged in place for several seconds, tried putting my hair in a ponytail, looked at it in the mirror above the entryway table and changed my mind, wrapped the hair tie around my wrist in case I wanted it later, and headed back to my room to grab my phone. In the past two days, I had spent nearly every waking moment, and even my sleeping and dreaming moments, thinking about this one single meeting with my dad. Most of my thoughts focused on the details that didn't matter, like what to wear, how to greet him, whether I should act excited or casual when I said hello for the first time. Where would we go? Would we go to dinner? What if people recognized me and whispered about me, or worse, insulted me to my face? Every thought I had centered on my desire for his approval and my fear that he might be disappointed in me.

I tried to think about what Ginny might tell me. If she was here, she'd probably say something like, "Hey, if he's not nice to you, it's on him. He should be proud you're his daughter and thankful you reached out to him, so be confident." Funny how the words she might say popped easily into my mind. I did that a lot lately, thought about things through Ginny's view. It always made me feel better, and interestingly enough, the words I imagined she'd say also seemed like what God might say to me.

I checked my phone for the time—5:58, two minutes before I was supposed to hear that knock on the door. I continued to hear Grandma shuffling around, picking things up, putting dishes away in the kitchen. She wasn't one to sit and do nothing on a normal day, but this was Grandma to the extreme. She had vacuumed, dusted, picked wildflowers and placed them in jars and vases around the dining and living rooms. She waved sage leaves in the air as she walked around and prayed. She sang even more than normal, which is a lot, but this time her voice seemed tense, crackly, nervous. It was usually smooth and calming. I wished Jared were home, but he was still at basketball practice. He would have helped me feel better.

"How are you doing?" Grandma asked as she entered my room and smiled in a way that looked more afraid than happy.

"I'm okay," I said, "a bit nervous."

"Well, that's to be expected. Just remember, your father is lucky to have a daughter like you. Be yourself and don't worry."

I laughed a little, surprised at how she echoed my thoughts. "Thanks, Grandma. I was just thinking Ginny might say that if she were here."

She smiled and nodded. "Oh yes, that Ginny is a smart one. She would say that."

Grandma stood in the doorway and continued to gaze at me, like she was trying to read my thoughts.

"Is there anything I can do or get you? I know it's about time now."

"I'm fine, thanks. I'll be out there in a minute."

When Grandma left, I double-checked myself in the mirror, brushed my hair for the third time, debated which sweatshirt to bring in case it got chilly, chose the light blue one and held it in my lap as I sat on the bed and checked the time again—6:02. That didn't bother me much at first. A couple minutes late was no big deal, but as a couple minutes became 30 minutes, 40 minutes, 60 minutes, I officially felt a bit crazy inside. I had moved to the dining room, then to the living room, and then paced from room to room because I couldn't sit still. Also, it was easier to be in whatever room Grandma wasn't singing and praying in.

At 7:05, I sent him a text message. *Everything okay? You said 6:00, right?*

Then I waited for a response. And waited. And waited.

The sadness I felt was compounded by the sad look on Grandma's face every time she looked at me and asked, "Everything okay? Heard from your dad yet?"

She had asked at least three times, which is reasonable, but I hated telling her the same answer. "Yeah, everything's okay, but I haven't heard from him."

The second part of that answer was the truth, but the first part really wasn't. I didn't know how to tell her how I really felt. It was hard enough to feel it quietly. Speaking it aloud would make it too real, too final, too harsh. But the truth was, everything was not okay. He wasn't coming. And the bigger truth was, I had a father who didn't care about me.

# –37–

Grandma took Jared and me out to get hamburgers, fries, and shakes for dinner the night my dad didn't show up.

"Order anything you want darling," Grandma said, "And if I were you, I'd make sure to get a chocolate shake too. Not much better than that for comfort food."

I stared at the menu on the wall while Jared placed his order first. I tried to will what I was thinking out of my mind, to force it to go away by thinking simply about the goodness of a shake as far as flavor and satisfaction goes, but all I could think of was the fact that Mom would have said the exact same thing Grandma did. In fact, that day in sixth grade when I was made fun of for my homemade clothes, she saw I was sad, and although I hadn't told her why, she assumed I had first day blues and deserved a treat. So we went to the nearest drive-thru that day, ordered two shakes and two large fries, headed to a park, sat by the pond there and watched the ducks. All my troubles had left me for a while as I watched those ducks waddle about, paddle through the water, race each other for food they found.

So in an attempt to feel better about my father, I robotically asked for a chocolate shake and nothing else. After we sat down at one of two open tables, waiting for our food, the thought of a shake arriving made me ache inside, but not out of hunger. I missed my mom horribly, and in spite of how thankful I was for Grandma trying to cheer me up, and for Jared's hand on mine, I couldn't shake my sadness over her not being there. The more I thought about her and the fact that my father wanted nothing to do with me, the more anger I felt. Tears filled my eyes. *Think of something else, Emily. Don't do it. Do not cry.*

The tears came rushing out. Those reckless, disobedient beads of moisture that announced all my pain streamed down my face.

"Uhhhh!" I pressed my hands against my face, wiped the tears, and slammed my hand on the table. "I hate being so sad all the time!"

The low murmur of conversation in the restaurant stopped, and I saw all eyes on me. Now I was sad *and* embarrassed. Grandma grabbed my hands and held them in hers. One of the good things about being called crazy all the time was she could really care less about anyone looking at her. The more I saw that in her, the more I wanted to be like that.

"Listen, Emily dear, you have every right to be angry right now about feeling sad. You don't deserve any of this. I wish I could wave my hands and make it all go away. But even though I can't do that, I know I can pray for you to feel God with you in all this. It would be nice if we were promised happy and problem-free lives, but unfortunately we live in a broken world that goes against God. So when this bad stuff hits, we have to remember it's not from him. He is sad for you too right now, so he will give you strength. He will help you."

I really wanted to believe that. I was tired of relying on anyone else, like my own parents, to help me feel happy. Grandma helped. Jared helped. But I still felt sad. I needed strength from something more powerful.

"I hope that's true, Grandma. I don't know if I believe it, but I want to."

She smiled and squeezed my hand. "That's the first step, wanting to believe. Pray, give it some time."

The cashier called our number, and Jared jumped up in response. "I'll get that." He was probably relieved to break away from all the emotion of Grandma and me. Plus, he was undoubtedly even more excited to be eating something with decent amounts of fat and grease instead of Grandma amounts of vitamins and nutrients.

Jared gave me a handful of his fries, told me I needed to eat more than a shake. I picked up a french fry, dipped it in the ketchup cup, then swirled it around on the paper hamburger wrapper. I drew a heart, then wiped it out with the fry, dipped it again, drew a happy face, or at least tried to. After looking at it, I realized it probably looked more like the way I felt inside, all smudged, the smile not really a smile, just a red blob. I took one sip of the shake. It didn't taste as good as I remembered.

We normally talked at least a little at dinner, but I didn't even feel like trying to start a conversation. Small talk about all the dumb things that didn't matter like weather, or school, seemed like a waste of energy, and I definitely didn't feel like talking about all the things in my life that did matter. But of course, Grandma wasn't going to let us all sit in silence.

"You know, when I was a kid and my parents would take my sister and me out for food, we always ended up bringing a bunch of this stuff home with us," she said.

"Let me guess. It was too much unhealthy stuff, so you only ate part of it?" Jared said, obviously trying to be funny.

Grandma smiled and waved a fry in the air as she responded. "No, no. My parents weren't really into healthy food, so I didn't mean the food. My father was, however, into saving anything else he thought he might need later. Those ketchup cups, for example, he'd ask for a bunch of them, like ten, put all but the one he used into his pocket, and then go up and ask for more before we left. He'd grab handfuls of napkins too, which would all go into the paper bag the food came in, and straws, lots of straws. These would all go home with us and sit on top of all the other stacks and stacks of saved junk he kept and wouldn't get rid of. If you thought I was crazy for collecting things, you should have seen him."

Jared gulped a bite of hamburger, slurped his soda quickly and said with his eyes wide, "Whoa, so he was like one of those hoarders you see on television?" Jared asked.

Grandma raised an eyebrow, her mouth full, nodded as she finished chewing. "Yes, he was a hoarder. He saved everything. Our house was filled to the brim with anything you could ever possibly need, or not need. It became pretty embarrassing. After I had my first few friends over, they never seemed to want to come back. I thought everyone's house was like ours until I went over to my friend Nancy's house. I couldn't believe how much space she had. It was so open and roomy. I could see the placemats on the table, set and ready for dinner to be served. I saw the color of the floor in every room and the pictures on the wall. I could walk freely without having to meander a maze of boxes and stacks of magazines, paper towels, canned goods. It was incredible. It only took one more visit to another person's house, our neighbor, for me to begin to understand we weren't normal. Plus, I heard people say things about me and how my house was a pit. So I stopped inviting anyone over."

"Well that's sad," Jared said. I agreed, even though I hadn't found it in me to talk yet.

"Yes, well, that wasn't the worst of it though." She wiped her mouth, and paused for a moment. I noticed her fingers, nervously tapping the table. I searched in my head for a way to tell her she didn't have to say any more, but she began again before I thought of anything. "My mother was really the tough one to live with. She didn't have a problem with saving things, but she sure knew how to store up anger and resentment, then unload it with such force that I was glad I had stacks of things to hide behind." She wouldn't look at us as she said this. She kept her eyes down and fiddled with her straw wrapper, twisting it into a thin spiral, then tearing it into tiny pieces.

Now I had to say something. "Grandma, I'm so sorry. That's horrible." I put my hand on her nervous fingers.

"Yeah, it really is. I'm sorry," Jared said and put his hand on both of ours.

She looked up and into my eyes, then at Jared. "It's okay," she smiled gently. "I'm not telling you this to make you feel bad. I'm telling you so you see that parents mess up sometimes. They aren't always equipped to love you the way you deserve to be loved. I let the fact that my parents were unstable and unkind get to me for a long time. I even felt guilty for being upset with them after they treated me badly. But then I learned that isn't from God. You both need to know that you are not the sum of what others say or how they treat you. You are worth everything to God. He is your true father, and you are his beloved children, always. That's all that matters."

I could see clearly in Grandma's eyes she believed that. I hoped someday I could believe that too.

# 38

After a pep talk like Grandma gave, you'd think I would have felt empowered, thankful that someone loved me enough to tell me all those things. But over the course of the week, I kept feeling sad. Every little thing seemed to remind me that my life was a mess.

School was one of those things. I had spent so much free time focusing on my grandparents, my dad, and of course, Ginny, that I hadn't done much homework or studying. Some people could maybe get away with that, but not me. I was the type of student who did well because I worked hard. If I didn't, it showed. So after three failed quizzes and a D on a test, I felt lost. Everything seemed hard, especially friends, or the lack of them I should say. I got to see Jared at lunch, so that was nice. But one day he had a basketball meeting, and that's when I realized how alone I felt without him or Ginny.

I grabbed my lunch from my locker and went to the grassy area where Jared and I usually ate. I tried to be positive, thinking the alone time would give me time to study for my next class where I had a history test. I sat down, opened my book, and stared at the page in front of me. I began reading the section titled *The Impact of the French Revolution*, but my mind wandered to my dad, my mom. What were they doing right now? Why did I care? Did they think about me? What was Ginny doing? Would everything go okay on prom night? I looked up, dumb idea, and noticed my least favorite crowd from English class huddled on some benches glancing my direction. Cameron eyed me, leaned in to her huddle of followers to say something. Then they all looked at me and laughed. I wanted to stand up and tell her to talk to me face to face, tell her she was a coward, but instead, I put my head down and pretended to focus on the uprising in France, King Louis XVI, Napoléon.

When lunch finally ended, I remembered nothing I had read, and so continued to bomb another test. Track practice was next, and after the warm up I already felt exhausted. I fell behind in every interval, got a side cramp about half way in, and finally asked Coach Tino if I could leave because I wasn't feeling well.

"Yeah, I was thinking you were looking a bit weak out there," he said. I knew he didn't mean that in an unkind way, but hearing it made me feel like a huge failure.

"Sorry, I don't mean to be a letdown," I said, fighting back tears.

"Hey, don't ever say that about yourself," he said. "You're not feeling your best. It happens. Go get some rest and come back stronger next time. I know you're not a quitter."

I nodded my head and looked away from him. I knew if I looked at him and spoke what I was thinking, I would lose it. The truth was, I wanted to quit. I wanted to go home, lay in my room and stay there for days. I was tired of trying to be happy, trying to look like I was okay. It was exhausting. "Thanks," I managed to say.

The fact that he was so nice was comforting, but also troubling. I wasn't used to coaches giving any sympathy for simply not feeling well. I'd seen them be nice, but only when someone was really struggling, like my friend Tammy from back home. Last year her mom had a sudden stroke and was hospitalized. Tammy was fine for a couple days, would be next to me or right behind me on every run, as usual. But one day she lagged behind everyone. She looked really weak and sad. The coach told her almost the same thing as Coach Tino did to me, to go home and rest. She ended up being out for the entire week, and when she did come back she was like a different person. She didn't try, she'd stop and walk all the time. She had given up. So, what bothered me was I obviously looked horrible. I wasn't hiding my feelings anymore. I wasn't fighting through it, and I'd pretty much always been able to do that. I was afraid I wouldn't get my strength back, that this was the end of track for me.

I normally didn't mind walking home after practice. But today, I wasn't in the mood. I thought about calling Jared to pick me up, but I didn't feel like talking to anyone, not even him.

I didn't bother to look around and enjoy anything around me while I walked. I stared at the ground, the black asphalt of the road, the dirt path, weeds. I just wanted to be done with this day. When I finally got home, I was relieved that Grandma was napping, and Jared was in his room, the door closed. I went straight to my bedroom, plopped onto the bed, and looked up at the ceiling. I knew I was about to cry, so looking at nothing was all I wanted to do. But of course, once I glanced around the room, all I saw was my mother, all the little bits and pieces of her childhood basically shouting at me for attention—her stuffed animals, the clothes in her closet, her artwork, and that photo of her and my dad. That's the one that did it. Every tear I'd been holding back came rushing out.

With tears rolling down, I stood up, grabbed the photograph, walked down the hall into the kitchen, and threw it in the trash. Then I stomped back.

"Emily dear, is that you?" I heard Grandma say, half asleep.

"Yes," I continued to head back to my room and shut the door. I hoped Grandma would leave me alone. I knew she'd be wondering why I didn't say much to her and was hiding in my room, but I didn't care. I was too depressed to worry about her feelings. I looked at my mom's prom dress, hanging prominently on my closet door, and glared at it. Storming toward the dress, I tore it down and flung it across the room just as Jared entered.

"Hey," he said with a surprised look, "What's going on?"

He had that concerned and scared puppy dog look he used to give Mom when she was upset and paced around the house. The fact that he looked at *me* this way made me lose it even more.

"What's going on?" I shouted. "Oh nothing, nothing at all. I'm just failing all my classes, have no friends, no parents. That's all. Everything is pretty normal and great!"

I plopped down on the floor, leaned back against my bed. The crumpled dress on the floor looked better there. It didn't deserve to be on display, nor did that picture, reminding me of my smiling parents who could care less about me.

Jared came over and sat next to me, put his hand on mine. "I get it, Em. I get why you're mad."

He didn't say any more, but put his arms around me and pulled me close, and through tears I let everything out.

"I can't imagine putting on that dress that makes me look even more like my mom, when she was happy with my dad. I want to forget about them." I pressed my hands on each side of my head, the pressure making the throb of an oncoming headache feel better. "Plus, a prom at the hospital is nothing like the real thing, and let's be honest, it's my fault Ginny can't go to the real thing. Who am I kidding by trying to make this a happy occasion?"

"Okay, first off, it's not your fault. You need to stop thinking that. But also, we don't have to do this prom thing. We can do something else. We can go see Ginny with jeans on and have a party, not even call it prom. You know her, she'll love it no matter what because you're there, and so will I. I asked you to prom because I thought you wanted to go. I remembered you and Ginny talking about it all the time, and when I asked you, you were so happy. But if it makes you sad, we should do something different."

I relaxed into his arms and responded in the only way I could right then. "Thank you, Jared. Thank you." For the first time all day, I was thankful for something. I was so lucky to have him. *Thank you, God, for Jared,* I prayed, thinking that maybe God was telling me my life wasn't a complete mess.

# –39–

"Emily? Jared?" Grandma entered the room, hand on her hip.

We both looked up at her, but said nothing. She walked over and sat down on the floor with us. Once she was at our level, I saw something in her hand. It was the photograph, and now I also noticed the look on her face. She did not look pleased.

"So, I found this in the trash," she began. She looked momentarily at Jared and then fixed her gaze on me. "I understand if you don't want to think about your parents right now. They have not made good choices at all, and they have hurt you deeply." She looked away from me and down at the picture. Then she took a deep breath as she looked at me again. "But you can't toss them away." Tears filled her eyes. "They have hurt me as well, but I refuse to think there's no hope for them or our relationship, and being angry at them actually does more harm to you than them, Emily."

I felt horrible. I didn't mean to hurt Grandma. I didn't even think about her finding the picture or asking about it, which showed that I didn't think at all. I simply acted out of anger.

"I'm sorry, Grandma."

"I understand, Emily. I really do. But I'm going to keep the picture. It doesn't need to be in here. I'll keep it in another room."

She started to get up.

"Wait, what did you mean it's more harmful to me than them? It kind of made me feel better to throw that in the trash." I hoped this wouldn't make her angry to hear, but I really did want to know what she meant.

She stood up and said, "Wait one minute. I think a rock might be a good way to explain this."

*Oh my, not again*, I thought. Hadn't she already told me a story involving a rock?

She returned with a stone much bigger than the tiny one she'd spoken about before. This one filled her hand, about the size of a tennis ball. She sat down and held it in front of her. It was black with tiny white speckles on it.

"Okay, so here it is. I think you know about Jesus dying on the cross to forgive our sins. But sometimes we know that and don't really understand how much it means for us every single day. I want you to look at this rock and imagine one so much bigger, one about the size of this entire wall." She pointed to the bedroom wall. "A stone at least that size, weighing tons, blocked the tomb where Jesus lay. But when the women went to the tomb the day after Jesus was crucified, the stone had been rolled away. Confused and upset, they went inside the tomb, and saw that the body of Jesus was gone. While they stood there puzzled, two angels appeared, saying Jesus had risen, that his promise to die and return to life had come true."

She looked at Jared and me with a glimmer in her eye. She loved these stories, and by now I did too. Now that I had learned they actually meant something, and that she wasn't really a crazy person, I listened better.

She continued. "So that huge stone, when moved away, showed us that Jesus didn't die on the cross for nothing. He died so we could be forgiven, and then rose to life. He set us free. When we don't forgive, it's like we have this heavy stone on our hearts. We are asked to forgive others because we have been forgiven, so when we don't, we are like that closed tomb, trapped by our own bitterness and anger. When you stay mad at your mom and dad, or anyone, you are basically keeping yourself imprisoned, Emily. You're about as free as your mom is behind those bars. You have to move that stone away and trust God. Let it go and move forward."

She was sort of making sense, but I was still not sure how to move on. "I see what you're saying, but I don't know how to magically stop being mad. That feels impossible."

"It probably is impossible on your own, Em. You need God to help you. You need to rely on him all the time, and eventually it will get better. You might still have days where you feel upset or sad, but then you have to lean on him even more."

I didn't know how that would work, but I wanted to believe her. I really wanted to be better inside.

"I'm going to give you this rock, Emily." She grabbed my hand and placed the rock in it. It appeared to be a difficult thing for her to give. "I've had this rock since my last disagreement with my parents, where they stopped speaking to me. This rock has always reminded me to forgive them and others. It has also reminded me of where I can find strength. It's not in any one person or thing. I've told you several Bible verses about rocks that are favorites of mine. The one I learned when I decided to keep this rock is from Psalm 18. It says, 'I love you, Lord; you are my strength. The Lord is my rock, my fortress, and savior; my God is my rock, in whom I find protection. He is my shield, the power that saves me, and my place of safety.'" Tears rolled down her cheeks. "I don't need this stone to remind me of that anymore, so I pass it on to you, my dear Emily."

I've never received a better gift, a simple stone, wrapped in love and hope.

# 40

I slept with that rock by my bed, next to the mustard seed necklace Grandma had given me, and woke up the next morning happy to see it. To anyone else it would appear to be an ordinary rock, but to me, it was more like a precious gem, a rare find. It obviously meant a lot to Grandma, and she gave it to me. If there was anyone I wanted to be more like, it was her, and if she found her strength in God, I thought maybe I should too.

I picked up the rock and sat up in my bed. I saw the crumpled dress still on the floor across the room, reminding me that today was prom. I thought back to that day Jared asked me to go. I was so happy. I remembered the look on Jared's face when he saw me in my mom's dress. I wanted to feel like I did then. I hated who I had been the past couple days.

I remembered Ginny's excitement about bringing the prom to her, and the look on Mrs. Bartle's face. If anyone had reason to be mad at me for her daughter sitting in a hospital on prom night, it would be her. But she never acted mad at me. She treated me like I was her daughter, and she'd been working hard to make this night special. We couldn't show up in jeans and spoil all she had done, or risk disappointing Ginny.

I sat up, eyeing the dress that seemed to be shouting at me

to pick it up from the floor. I walked over, held it up, and looked in the mirror. I pictured myself with my hair done, high heels strapped on, laughing with Ginny, Chris, and Jared. I knew I'd regret it if I backed out.

I placed the dress on my bed, and headed to the kitchen where I heard Jared commenting on Grandma's cooking.

"This is so awesome, wow, so good," I heard him say.

"Oh, thank you dear. I'm so glad you like it," Grandma responded.

I entered to see Jared digging into a plate full of waffles. Next to him was also a bowl of fruit and a heaping plate full of bacon. He didn't see me in the doorway, so I stood and watched for a moment. He was definitely not one to hide when he enjoyed something. In spite of a mouth full of food, he still managed a smile, and he leaned over the plate with a fork in one hand, knife in the other, prepped to dive in again. It was incredible how much he could eat.

"Just a light breakfast to start your day?" I asked him with a smile.

He glanced up, opened his eyes wide with delight, and nodded his head. After a big swallow he said, "Yes, this is the best, but I'd call it brunch. You do realize how late you slept, right?"

Before I could come back with a comment about how late he usually slept, Grandma asked, "Oh, hello dear, would you like some?"

"Uh, yes, if there's enough. I don't want to leave this guy starving for more."

Grandma laughed. "Oh, that won't be a problem. I made a lot."

I looked at the dish she was holding with stacks of waffles and bacon left.

"Wow, yes, looks like you're serving at least ten of us. Keep going, Jared. You've got some work to do," I said.

"Oh, don't worry, none of it will be wasted," he said with a wide grin.

"Well, as long as you can fit into that tux still, it's fine with me."

I didn't think anything could slow down his frenzied eating, but that did. He froze mid bite, set his fork and knife down, and stared at me.

"What do you mean fit into a tux? Are you saying you want to stick with our original plan?" His grin hadn't left his face. He was really like a little kid when he was excited about something. I loved that about him.

"Yes? If you still want to go?" I asked, a bit worried he thought I was the most unpredictable and emotional person ever.

He still didn't say anything, but stood up, walked over to me, and pulled me into a big hug. I knew this meant "yes", he wanted to go, and it also meant he cared about me in spite of my crazy moods.

"I'm glad you're smiling again," he said as he pulled away, "So yes, I want to go."

After we ate, Jared went to pick up his tux and shoot hoops at the park, while I conquered the many tasks of getting ready. I took a long shower, smothered my face with a mask of avocado, oatmeal, and honey that Grandma promised was great for moisturizing and detoxifying my skin before I put all that makeup on. I gave myself a manicure and pedicure, washed the mask off, applied concealer, blush, and mascara, dried my hair, curled it, practiced putting it up three different ways, decided to keep it down, curled it again, tousled it, decided it was good. By the time I pulled the dress on, strapped on the heels I found in Grandma's closet that fit me and didn't look like a Grandma shoe, Jared was already sitting in the other room. It had taken him about twenty minutes to get ready.

I gazed into the mirror and saw Grandma step behind me. She beamed with a big smile.

"You look beautiful. You always do, but today it's different. You look truly happy."

"Thanks, Grandma," I glanced down at my dress, a little surprised by how much I liked it now after all the rage it spurred in me yesterday. "I actually feel happy. Do you want to take a picture of us?"

She snapped out of her dreamy gaze, but held her warm smile. "Oh, yes, I do. Let's go get Jared." She grabbed my hand, ready to pull me toward the bedroom door.

"Oh, no, I do want one with Jared, but right now I was talking about you and me. We don't have any pictures together."

Grandma's eyes welled up with tears. "Oh, well, yes. That would be wonderful, but I'm not really dressed for the occasion."

"You're dressed perfectly, Grandma, come here."

She stood next to me, and I held up my phone to take a selfie of us. We both looked at it after.

"Oh, I really like that," she said. I liked it too. We both looked truly happy, for the first time in a long time.

When Jared saw me, he didn't move. He stared at me, shook his head and said, like he had before, "Wow."

Wow had a whole new meaning for me now. It was a small, simple word, but it said a lot.

Grandma took several pictures of us, in the living room, then outside under the tree, reminding me of the day all I saw here was dirt and dust, thinking it was ugly. I couldn't imagine it any better now.

"Hold on, I forgot something." I trotted as well as I could in my heels back inside, then down the hall to the bedroom. The rock was still sitting next to my bed, along with the mustard seed necklace. I put the necklace on, not caring whether it looked funny doubled with Mom's elegant beads. *Yep, I'm definitely learning to embrace a little bit of crazy*, I thought. I grabbed the rock next and then went into Grandma's room, where the picture of my mom and dad sat on her nightstand. I stared at the picture and then held it to my chest along with the rock. *Forgive, Emily. Let it go.*

I slipped the photo into my purse, and then the rock. I checked the mirror one more time. The girl I saw looking back at me was still the same girl on the outside, all dressed up, looking a lot like her mom, but inside she was becoming free, light, and finally herself.

# ACKNOWLEDGMENTS

The expression, "It takes a village to raise a child" is the one that comes to mind when I think of this book. It has literally taken a village to get this "baby" raised and launched into the reading world.

First and foremost, I am thankful to God, who has put the desire to write in my heart since I was a child, gifted me with the opportunity and courage to let others read my words, and never leaves my side.

I am so thankful for my family, who listened to me repeat year after year that I was going to publish my novel. You never laughed at me, or mocked me. You simply kept encouraging and telling me you believed in me, and now that I've achieved it, you continue to cheer me on.

Thank you to my wonderful friends, those I've known since childhood and those I've met as an adult, fellow teachers, co-workers, pastors, parents of my children's friends, Revelation Wellness friends. I wish I could name every single one of you because you each have a piece of my heart.

Thank you to my students, who have inspired me more than you probably know. Your stories, both real-life and written, have shaped my story. You have reminded me to be courageous, to share the good and the bad, to be willing to accept criticism, and to never give up on a dream. You are wonderful fans and wonderful people.

Thank you to those who have shaped and encouraged my writing over the years: my teachers, like Mrs. Ledbetter who told me way back in 5th Grade that I was a good writer, literary agent Tony Lopopolo, for your honest feedback and encouragement on this novel from its very early stages, author Michelle Richmond, who not only edited and critiqued my first draft, helping me make many needed changes, but also took the time to meet me for coffee and encourage me to send this novel forth into the publishing world. I hope my words can come close to the beauty and impact of yours. Also, Carolyn McGrath, for your integral feedback on my early draft. I am blessed by you as an editor and mother-in-law.

Last but not least, to Acorn Publishing, who took this tiny acorn of a manuscript and helped it grow into the little oak of a published book. Holly Kammier, you are the most amazing editor. I am so grateful for all your time with my book. Jessica Therrien, thank you for patiently answering my many questions and for guiding me in this entire process. Debra Kennedy, thank you for your amazing gifts and patience with formatting and editing. Thank you also to all the fellow Acorn writers, who have welcomed and supported me. I feel blessed to be a part of this amazingly talented group.

# ABOUT THE AUTHOR

Dianne Beck has spent the majority of her career teaching students ranging from Kindergarten through adult. No matter what age, her biggest goal is to encourage her students to be their own unique selves, to have confidence in who they are, and to follow their passions.

Dianne's debut young adult novel Sticks and Stones was inspired by her years of teaching, where she saw so many students struggle with varying issues, and also experienced how an understanding ear and relevant literature could make a significant impact on their lives. She hopes young people as well as adults can find faith and strength, like her main character Emily did, even when things seem to be falling apart.

Dianne is motivated daily by her faith in God, her husband, and her four adult children. When she's not writing, she can be found reading, sipping coffee, browsing a bookstore, or pursuing a part-time faith and fitness ministry at ofcommonground.com.

You can visit her author website at diannebeck.com.

Made in the USA
Middletown, DE
24 March 2022

63060434R00137